Where the Money Went

NAN A. TALESE
DOUBLEDAY

NEW YORK
LONDON
TORONTO
SYDNEY
AUCKLAND

Where the Money Went

Stories

Kevin Canty

Copyright © 2009 by Kevin Canty

All rights reserved. Published in the United States by Nan A. Talese, a division of Random House, Inc., New York and in Canada by Random House of Canada Limited, Toronto.
www.nanatalese.com

DOUBLEDAY is a registered trademark of Random House, Inc. Nan A. Talese and the colophon are trademarks of Random House, Inc.

Some of the stories in this book have appeared, in different form, in the following publications: "They Were Expendable" in *Tin House*, "In the Burn" in *Chattahoochee Review*, "Sleeping Beauty" in *Glimmer Train*, and "The Boreal Forest" in *H.O.W. Journal*.

Book design by Elizabeth Rendfleisch

Library of Congress Cataloging-in-Publication Data
Canty, Kevin.
    Where the money went : stories / Kevin Canty.
—1st ed.
        p. cm.
    1. Man-woman relationships—Fiction.
    2. Men—Psychology—Fiction. I. Title.
    PS3553.A56W47 2009
    813'.54—dc22
                            2008037480

ISBN 978-0-385-52585-5

PRINTED IN THE UNITED STATES OF AMERICA

10 9 8 7 6 5 4 3 2 1

First Edition

For Aryn

Contents

Where the Money Went

Where the Money Went

W H E N T H E T H I N G W A S O V E R , Braxton sat down at the kitchen table of his apartment and tried to figure out what they had done with the money.

Some of it went for schools, of course, good private schools— the hippy school for Lucinda and the Spanish Academy for Steve. The hippy school was a parent co-op. Braxton remembered sweating through a parent meeting, drunk: the affluent and lawyerly, trying out their voices on one another. On and on. It was like being in the eighth grade again, stupid with boredom, ready to flee. Plus the parent co-op was more expensive than the academy, ten thousand a year versus six. Plus the afterschool care. Plus Brenda, the sitter. The weekend art lessons, the tennis clinics, swimming.

Not that the public schools were terrible. They were fine.

Some of it went for cars, landscaping, clothes, vacations.

The four of them flew to Honolulu for Christmas, Vail for Presidents' Day. He sat with pencil and envelope-back (he was pre-approved for fifty thousand dollars more) and tried to figure how a simple skiing weekend could cost so much: lift tickets, lunches, the fat, hourglass-shaped skis he bought himself and then, out of something like guilt, bought his wife. It wasn't the skis he bought himself that were wasted, he thought. He was a decent skier, he enjoyed it. No, it was the skis he bought his wife, hoping to encourage her. She used them that weekend and never again. Five hundred for the skis, one-and-a-quarter for the bindings. Then of course new boots.

That was a waste, he thought.

The snorkeling equipment, the Windsurfer, the mountain bike. A Klein, he remembered. He had spent months researching what the absolute best kind to get was. The little crazy expensive bike he bought Steve so they could tool slowly around the playground on their thousand-dollar rides, father and son.

They threw a party when the pool was done. Everybody they knew, under the lights. Braxton spent a thousand dollars at the liquor store alone, not to mention the catering, the lights, the pool itself. And then she had gotten drunk, early in the evening, some accident where she had forgotten to eat. It didn't happen constantly or even often but she loved to be drunk. She raced around the pool in the shadowy light, chatting, flirting. She was standing with her back to the pool, talking with the Andersons, when she took that one slow inadvertent step backward and could not right herself. He watched her topple slowly backward into the water, watched her dress bloom around her in the underwater light like some bright colorful flower and in that moment he had not disliked her. In fact he loved her, just in that moment.

Then heard the whispered word: "drunk." It passed around him, hand to hand.

Then she got out and she didn't even care, she went around the rest of the night in her wet dress, her nipples poking through the wet cotton.

The parkas, stereos.

The afternoon he figured out how bad it was, how bad it was going to get, he was in their bedroom, which faced the pool. Looking up from his bills and figuring, he saw Steve bobbing in the deep end on a silver plastic raft, eyes closed, hours on end. He had turned fat with his tenth birthday—"husky," she called it. Every time Braxton looked up, his son was there, immobile, drifting. He gets it from her, he thought angrily. That indolence. He looked on his son with disgust.

The rest of the money, what there was of it, went for the lawyers.

The Emperor of Ice Cream

THE SUMMER HE ALMOST KILLED HIS BROTHER, Lander spent working at the front desk of the University library, watching the girls go by in their summer shorts and dresses. There was almost no traffic at the checkout counter, but the girls would come in early and late to check their e-mail at the long banks of computers, wearing wet bathing suits under their clothes sometimes. The girls all wore river sandals, and their feet were tan. It was hot all summer, months without rain or even clouds. In the cool and quiet of the library, Lander could feel the whole world outside having fun without him.

The doctors said the fact that Tim was drunk might have saved his life in the crash. And Lander was definitely the one who should have been driving that night: he passed the Breathalyzer and the blood test both, though not by much. It didn't matter. It wasn't like his parents called a family meeting to announce they didn't like him anymore. But they weren't pestering him to come home every weekend. They had troubles of their own.

His sister, Jen, was in and out of town that summer, too, finishing up the last three credits of her English teaching certificate. Jen would go up to Bigfork on Friday and come back Sunday, while Lander worked his weekend job at the ice-cream store, but she never had much to say to him when she got back. Lander was under the impression that she spent most of her time at the lake working on her tan. Their parents had split up that spring, and their father was then living on a forty-two-foot power boat tied up to the dock by Marina Cay, directly under the windows of their former condo, where his mother still lived. At least this is what Lander heard. He hadn't gotten up to see it yet.

Day after day after day rose into the nineties and stayed there till evening. The sun was always shining hard and the sky was an even cloudless blue. The library was always quiet and cool and lined with pretty girls who wanted nothing to do with him. At night, those same girls would come to the Orpheum, the ice-cream store, for tangerine sorbet and yellow-cake and bubble-gum cones. They would stand under the lights and lick their cones and laugh while Lander scooped another order out of the freezers with cold, chapped hands. Bugs circled and buzzed around the overhead lights. Summer was out there, out in the night.

* * *

T H E N , halfway through August, the call came that Tim was coming home from the nursing home in Kalispell.

Lander was supposed to drive up with his sister but he had to work till five that Friday. Jen went up at noon without him. The bank clock, when he finally got out of town, read 102 degrees, and the AC in his car didn't work right. He slugged his way north through twenty miles of the most major big-time road construction in the history of the world, stuck behind an elephant train of Winnebagos, as the dust blew in through the windows and settled on the dash. At times he would roll the windows up and pretend to be cool. By the time he got to Bigfork he was so air-dried, dusty and parched that his first steps carried him across the parking lot, down the dock and in one motion into the cold clean waters of the lake.

A delicious blinding cold went through him all at once in the cold lake-water, a dangerous bliss. He stayed underwater for as long as he could, rinsing the heat and dust out completely. When he surfaced and shook the water out of his eyes, he saw his father before him, standing next to some weird-looking neighbor kid on the deck of the largest motorboat Lander had ever seen. The lettering across the stern read LUCKY ME. His father was wearing a hat with a long birdlike bill and a complicated shirt with many flaps, pockets and buttons. In his salt-and-pepper beard, he did not look quite like Hemingway.

"Aren't you going to say hello to your brother?" his father asked him.

At first Lander didn't understand, then, dawning on him, he looked again at the weird-looking neighbor kid, who he had taken to be a twelve-year-old, and saw that it was actually Tim, or some small shrunken version of him. He looked tiny, thin and frail, and Lander felt a pang of fear run through him at the damage done.

"Jesus Christ," said Lander. "Get in the water."

Tim grinned down at him and it was actually him, just smaller and more tired. He asked, "Is that your wallet?"

Lander touched his back pocket underwater, and it was certainly his wallet. His father noticed. Tim laughed.

"Dumbass," Tim said.

"Actually, it's pronounced *Dumas*," Lander told him. He swam to the ladder on the side of the boat and clambered out, dripping, to man-hug his brother there. He was so small now! And pale, almost transparent.

"That is one big boat," Lander said to his father, who waited on deck.

"I'd forgotten," his father said, shaking his hand in his oversized burly way. "You haven't seen it yet. Let me give you the tour."

Behind his father on the rear deck of the boat, a pair of unnaturally good-looking tanned people sat in matching deck chairs, beaming at him. They were somewhere in their forties or even early fifties but they both looked fit and rested and eager—like eager golden retrievers held under restraint, Lander thought. He was afraid they were going to jump up and lick him.

"Steve and Polly Langendorf," said his father. "This is my son Lander."

They waited for him in their chairs and Lander was suddenly aware, as he shook their hands, that he was dripping wet and pale and a little fat, almost, from his nowhere summer. His mother looked down from the flying bridge overhead and shyly said hello. His *mother*! Last time he checked, Dad had a girlfriend and Mom had a lawyer.

"Tough trip up?" she asked. "Hi, sweetie. You look exhausted."

"I'm all right," Lander said. Just the fact that they had all been there together and he had not been invited, it left a weird taste in his mouth, like pennies or artichokes. OK, he had been invited, but not long ago. How long had this been going on?

"This is really something," Lander said.

"Twin Chryslers," his father said, as they passed through the living room and wheelhouse. "If you can afford to feed the beast, this thing will really go."

Belowdecks, evidence of careless male living was strewn around: laundry, dishes, the Telecaster that Lander had never quite learned to play and Tim had given up on, too. There was a picture of this same boat in a frame on the wall of the main cabin, which brought that taste into Lander's mouth again. It was just creepy, was all. The whole thing.

"I'm hungry," said his sister from somewhere nearby. He still hadn't seen her.

"We waited dinner for you," said his father—like this was something special, something other than the everyday congress of life. And here was his father's gigantic unmade bed in the rearward berth! For a moment, Lander wished himself back in the cool and quiet of the library, where things made sense. True, he was miserable there, but at least he knew why.

"And here's the guest quarters," said his father, leading him up to the slanted V-berth all the way forward, under the skylights, where two beautiful girls in tiny bathing suits were buffing their toenails. True, one of them was his sister, Jen, but one of them was not.

"Hey," said Lander.

"Hey," said his sister, without looking up.

"Hey," said the other girl. She smiled up briefly, insincerely, then went back to her work, but not before Lander saw she was pretty, polished but indifferent. She had the kind of lazy, languorous fog around her that Lander liked in a girl. Maybe there was something there for him.

"You're staying up in the condo," said his father. "Tim'll show you what's what. I'm going to go fire up the Weber."

Lander looked back wistfully at the two girls in their swimsuits but they were heads down, intent, elsewhere. His father led him up the passageway to where his brother waited on deck, under the eager gaze of the Langendorfs. Tiny, pale, frail.

"Who's the girl?" Lander asked on the way upstairs to the condo.

"One of the Langendorfs," Tim said. "Daughter of Ken and Barbie."

"I thought it was Steve and Polly."

"Whatever," Tim said.

"What's going on?" Lander said, when they got inside the condo hallway. A tomblike, air-conditioned quiet prevailed. "What the fuck, even. I mean, weren't they trying to kill each other when last seen?"

"It's an act," said Tim.

"And what's the deal with that fucking boat?"

"He's trying to sell the Inman place," Tim said, when they were into the condo. "He thinks he's got a shot at it with these two."

Lander set his bags down in the living room. The condo was unchanged since he last saw it, maybe since he first saw it, the clean quiet anonymity of a good hotel room. There was no sign of his mother's presence or his father's absence. He went to the refrigerator and took a cold beer, one of only three, he noted sadly. Beer run later. His brother was out on the little balcony, looking down at the little figure on the deck of the enormous boat. It dwarfed the other speedboats at the dock like a freighter in a yacht harbor.

"Dad thinks it'll go better if they can socialize them up," Tim said. "He's had a few things fall through this summer."

"Which one's the Inman place?"

"Over on Rocky Point?" Tim said. "We went by there once in the kayaks. It's the one with the fake waterfall."

"Geez," Lander said. "Two million?"

"Try eight," Tim said. "Things have been going crazy up here. That's the thing with the boat, Dad was going to buy a place for himself when he moved out, but every little rat shack with a dock is over a million. He couldn't find anything to buy."

"So he bought himself a private navy. What did that thing cost, anyway?"

"Cut him some slack," Tim said suddenly. "Both of them. It's been a tough summer."

Lander looked into his brother's face: small, hurt, closed. They were not in this together. They had always been before, always together.

"You want a beer?" Lander said. "Get you a beer?"

Again the closed, cloudy look in Tim's eyes. "I'm not supposed to," he said.

"OK," said Lander.

"I'm going to go downstairs, give Dad a hand," Tim said. "You go ahead and settle in."

Lander watched him leaving, getting ready to go, and felt a kind of panic to watch it. What was happening? They had never been like this before. He wanted to say something, anything, to keep Tim from going. In the end, he could only come up with "How are you doing, anyway?"

"I don't have a spleen anymore," Tim said. "I seem to get along without it just fine. That's about it. I don't miss that nursing home much."

"I'm sorry," Lander said.

"Don't worry about it," Tim said. "I don't imagine you did it on purpose."

He grinned at Lander in a hard cool way and left. Lander went out on the balcony again and looked down until he saw his brother set foot on the deck again, then turned back inside. Toy boat toy boat toy boat, he thought. The thing was three times the size of anything near it and gleaming white in the sun. Inside was the smell of perfumed soap and tears, his mother's house.

*   *   *

H E R name was Beth but she called herself Soleil, ever since she started at the University of Florida, which she admitted changing the name was a mistake, but it was too late to back out of. She was very stoned, as was Jen. She had braids in her hair with little beads at the end, and a widespread tattoo, just above her ass, which Lander had not managed to get a good look at yet. "How was I to know?" she said. "Straight out of high school in Dallas. Now I'm stuck with a stripper name. What's your stripper name?" she asked Lander.

"I didn't know I had one."

"The name of your first pet, then the first street you can remember living on."

"Ginger Fourth," he said.

"Ginger Forth!" said Soleil. "That's fucking awesome!"

"Ginger Osprey," said his sister, but this wasn't anywhere near as good, and they all knew it. A moment of silence followed, in which Lander smelled Judas on himself, to use his old love Ginger in such a way. She was a yellow Lab, shaded toward orange—an unusual color—who was tired and sweet and loved him unconditionally and showed it in her big tired eyes. All his life, Lander had tried to live up to the love of that dog, and now he had sold her out for a porn name.

"I want to go out," Soleil said. "I want to get drunk like a monkey, like a crazy little shithouse monkey."

"That can be done," said Tim. "That can be arranged."

They were the same age, Tim and Soleil, and they both had decent fake ID. Jen already had a date that night with her fiancé, Erik—another real-estate guy, a friend of her father's with nice teeth—which left Lander on the outside. Maybe. The four of them sat on the end of the dock at the state park, watching the sun go down across the lake. The hills on the far side were lion-colored and warm in the last of the sunlight and the lake was calm, dimpled with evening rises as the little fish came up to feed. Jen had brought a little bag of pot, which made her Soleil's best friend ever, and even Lander had a little buzz, which made him mopey and nostalgic. Once he and Tim had stood on this very dock and tried to catch those rising fish, before they realized that all those rises were really tiny fish, and not even worth catching.

"It's fucking awesome here," said Soleil.

The sun slid gently down under the Chief Cliffs on the far side, four miles of water away. When it was gone, a million stars came out at once, also a couple of high-flying planes and maybe a satellite. Lander thought it was, in fact, awesome, and there was nothing more to say.

Just then the *Lucky Me* steamed by, enormous and white and ghostly in the twilight.

"Where's he going?" Lander asked.

"Right now he's headed for the gas dock, it looks like," Tim said. "I think they're headed over to Lakeside for a drink later."

"A thousand dollars," Jen said.

"What?"

"That's what it takes to fill that thing up all the way," she said. "That's what Dad told me. Three two-hundred-gallon tanks. I saw Cameron Diaz in Lakeside last year."

"Shut the fuck up," said Soleil.

"Shopping for wine in the Lakeside IGA," Jen said. "She was with Christina Applegate. They both looked totally ripped."

"Get the fuck out of here," said Soleil.

"I'm one hundred percent not kidding," Jen said.

"Let's get out of here before he gets back," Tim said. "He's not going to like it much, me going out."

"You're not going anywhere," said Jen.

"I'm going to have, like, a Coke," Tim said. "I've been stuck inside that nursing home for six weeks. Besides, I feel fine."

"I'll get him home," said Lander.

Then they all remembered what happened the last time he said that, the last time he took Tim out. Not so good. Even to Lander, it just didn't feel right. Nothing was settled, nothing was done, and it wasn't even that long ago. He felt again the size of the thing, the awfulness.

"It's not a good idea," Jen said.

"Safe as houses," Lander said. "I'll have him in bed by eleven o'clock."

"Maybe," Tim said.

"I don't know a thing about this," Jen said. "I'm not hearing a word you say. Where are you heading, anyway?"

"We'll start off at the Garden Bar," Lander said. "Don't know after that."

"Don't say that! Bed after that. Bed!"

"We'll see," said Tim.

*   *   *

T H E Y would have made it undetected, except that Erik was waiting on the dock with the other grown-ups. Polly Langendorf was telling Lander's mother about Texas in the summer.

"I'm sure you've never been to Dallas," Polly said. "I'm sure you'd never want to go. But Dallas in the summertime is a special branch of hell."

"I've been to Houston several times," said Lander's mother.

"It's like living inside a cow's mouth," said Polly. "Between the heat and the pollution. This, on the other hand"—and here she swept her open hand across the horizon, where the setting sun made a bright edge along the tops of the hills, where the last light of day shined back at them on the water—"this is bliss."

"No humidity, either," said Steve Langendorf. "Plus the prices are still terrific."

"I could use a drink," said Lander's mother, to no one in

particular; then she spotted Lander, Tim and Soleil skulking down the edge of the dock. She stood, as if action were required.

"We're just going to walk downtown for a minute," Lander said. "We're going to show Soleil the bright lights of Electric Avenue."

"No you're not," said his mother.

"No what?" said Tim. "We're just going for a few minutes. It'll be fine."

"It's a terrible idea."

"No, it's fine," Tim said. "Don't worry. There's no need to worry."

And maybe it was the time of day and maybe it was the pot but Lander's little heart just turned blue to look at her. She was right and they were wrong and it didn't matter. They were going to leave anyway, just because they could, and she was going to sit and worry. That was the way it was with Lander's dad, too. People just did what they wanted to. Lander was the same way, too. He'd go downtown with his brother and the girl and later, when his brother went home, maybe he'd make a try for her. Maybe she'd be drunk by then. He looked at his mother and he smiled in a bright reassuring way.

"Everything's going to be fine," said Lander.

* * *

"I want a cowboy," said Soleil. "I'm going to get drunk as a monkey and I'm going to kiss a cowboy. That's the plan."

"It's not exactly cow country around here," Tim said.

"What kind of country is it?" she asked.

The brothers looked at each other. Really, the answer was lately that it was tourist country, tourists, skiers, hunting guides and real-estate agents. Everybody else was just making motel beds. The logging was long gone. But neither one of them had the stomach to tell her.

"The cows are about three hundred miles east of here," Lander said. "So are most of the cowboys."

"I've got a cowboy hat," Tim said. "I can run home and get it, if you want."

"You're too short," Soleil said, and took a long pull from her Long Island iced tea. Lander admired the workings of her neck as she swallowed, the well-groomed, well-tanned length of her. She really was a good-looking girl.

"I've got a pair of boots, too," Tim said. "I'm way taller in my boots. That's the cowboy's secret weapon."

It was a slow Friday night in the Garden Bar. Maybe it would pick up later. Maybe everybody was still at home, out on the deck, watching the stars appear out of the gathering dark of the sky, or maybe having an afterdinner shower to wash the sunblock and lake-water out of their hair. It didn't feel like that, though. It felt like it was going to stay Tuesday night forever, like the clocks were just going to stop and everybody stuck here in the same motions shooting pool, making small talk, feeding nickels into the video poker machine as the hands of the clocks rusted and fell away. That pot of Jen's was maybe better than he had given it credit for.

"This is *boring*," said Soleil.

"I'll shoot you a game of pool," Tim said.

"That's not boring?"

"It's boring in a different way," Tim said. "Come on."

Lander kicked back in his chair to watch them play. Like a lot of girls lately, especially the ones with money, she looked kind of fixed up and kind of trashy all at once. She wore big dangly earrings and a nice necklace, nice shoes, but her shirt was tiny and tight and her pants started way down low. After a couple of long shots, there wasn't much of a mystery about her tattoo anymore; it was a kind of Grateful Dead affair with wings and roses and a skull, arching over her butt, which was also worth regarding. He knew that women had the psychic power to know when someone was staring at their ass but he thought that Soleil probably didn't care. She wouldn't dress like that if she did; or maybe she would. It was a question he had been working over all summer.

"Dead," Soleil said.

"What?"

"This place is dead. There's got to be someplace better than this."

"It's early," Lander said.

"It's always something."

"We could try the Rusty Scupper," Tim said.

Lander looked at him long and discouragingly. The Rusty Scupper was not exactly a biker bar but there were usually a few parked out front. Plus it was eight or ten miles down the lakeshore, and he was not supposed to be driving anywhere with Tim in the car, not yet. He didn't know exactly what the rules were anymore but he knew this was one of them.

Also, and this was not anything he wanted to talk about, but wasn't Tim supposed to be getting on home soon? Lander thought the deal was, Tim would come out for a while, then they would walk him home and Lander would get his chance with Soleil, whatever that was. He wasn't optimistic, not at all, but he thought he was going to get a shot. Not with his brother hanging around, though.

"Who's driving?" he asked Tim.

"I will if you want me to," Tim said.

"You going to tell the folks?"

"They're out on the boat," Tim said. "I don't think they need to know every little detail. Besides, it's probably every little bit as dead down there as it is here."

"Don't tell me that," said Soleil. "I'd have to kill myself."

"Well, don't do that," Tim said. "I tried it and I didn't like it one damn bit."

"What was that all about?" she asked.

Which is how Lander found himself driving down Highway 35 in his new old pickup with Soleil riding bitch and Tim in the window seat, windows down, telling her his fascinating near-death story. The way Tim told about the accident, it was funny and mysterious and interesting, which was not at all the way Lander remembered it. It seemed to him to have been brutal and filthy and quick. He had turned left in front of a pickup truck he didn't see. It smashed into the passenger side, where Tim was sitting. Lander didn't remember a thing between that and the emergency room but Tim kept coming up with descriptive details of the event: the drunk housewife who found them and called the cops, the lights of the medevac helicopter through the trees. Lander didn't believe any of it but he didn't really mind a lie or two. Tim had all summer in the nursing home to make this shit up.

What he did mind was the way Soleil seemed to be taking it all in: avid, eager, a little greedy for the gory detail. "What happened to the guy?" she said. "The guy in the pickup, the one who hit you."

"He died," Tim said.

"Oh, shit," said Soleil; and then all three of them went quiet for a moment. Lander felt lost and lonely and sad and pissed. This wasn't Tim's story to tell. Not this part.

"Wasn't wearing his seat belt," Lander said. "Wife and three kids."

He had to say this, every time it came up. Otherwise it was just a story, something that happened. He needed to make it real, and saying this made it real. The wife's name was Barbara and the three kids were named Ellen, Susan and Mark.

"Shit," Soleil said quietly, and they drove the rest of the way to the bar without talking.

A band was playing at the Rusty Scupper when they got there, a country band you could hear perfectly well in the parking lot. Lander discovered a headache at the edge of his brain, sneaking up on him. Inside was overflowing with smoke and beer and shouted conversations, lots of hats and boots, which Lander thought would make Soleil happy. At this point, he was resigned to not getting any of the girl's attention, but it would please him no end if Tim didn't get any either.

"A shot of Jose Cuervo and a Corona," she said happily, once they were inside. "I'm going native!"

Lander said, "You're not going to go and get drunk on us, are you?"

"Fuck you, Ginger," said Soleil. "I was born drunk."

She waded off toward the bar, through the sweat and smoke, and both of the boys watched her go, as did several others. Her peekaboo tattoo.

"Ginger?" Tim asked.

"My porn name," said Lander.

"I thought it was Dumas," Tim said. "Guess I'll go get myself a drink, too."

"Don't do it," Lander said.

"Don't be such a candy ass," Tim said. "I paid five dollars to hear this crap band. I'm not going to just sit here with a Pepsi in my hand."

"You just got out of the hospital."

"Glad of it, too," Tim said. "Get you anything from the bar?"

Lander looked at him then but there was no way down from here. No way back. "Bottle of Bud, I guess," he said.

"That's more like it," Tim said, and was swallowed up by the crowd.

Bars: he used to be OK with them but not lately. The feeling had been coming and going all summer—Ellen, Susan and Mark—not entirely sadness, though sadness was part of it. Regret. Almost a sense of wonder, at how quickly things

could change, how little decisions snowballed into big differences, seconds became lifetimes. He looked at his hands,
still chapped from the hours at the Orpheum, and thought:
these were the hands that turned the wheel, without meaning
to, without trying for anything. He expected it would be bad
when he was alone, this feeling, but actually it had been coming at him worse when he was in crowds, like this one. These
were the moments where he felt cut off and stuck inside himself, looking out at the grinning, shouting crowd, smoking and
drinking, dancing and flirting away a summer night. Lander
thought they looked stupid. This was how he knew how fucked
up he was: when happy looked stupid.

He was OK when he was by himself, though. His little
station in the library. Dishing up cones to the girls in their
summer dresses.

Tim led the way back from the bar, blocking the drunks
out of the way for Soleil and her tray of drinks: three bottles of
Corona, six shots of tequila.

"Let's get this thing started," she said, setting the tray
down on a ledge, handing each of them a wedge of lime and
a shot. This was not going to end well, Lander knew it. He
looked over toward Tim but his brother ignored him, sucking the lime, tinking the shot glass against Soleil's and then
both of them downing the shot in one take. There was really
not much else to do but drink. Lander smiled at his brother in
what he hoped was a skeptical, distant way, then downed his
own shot. The tequila tasted like gasoline and burned all the

way down. He could feel it even afterward in his stomach, like a banked fire.

"And another," Soleil said, and she and Tim picked up their glasses and drank. They both looked at Lander.

"Not for me," he said. "Thanks."

"Well, I'm not going to fucking *waste* it," said Soleil, sweeping up the last shot and downing it as well. Which would be three shots in under three minutes. We'll see, Lander thought. Could be a short evening after all.

I'd like to settle down but they won't let me, sang the main guitar player, a short fellow in a tall hat. Soleil grabbed Tim and dragged him out onto the dance floor. Lander leaned against a wall and watched them twirl around. Maybe this would turn out all right after all. In the dim light of the bar, the sparkly Christmas lights over the stage had their own small magic. The crowd was a mix of everything, men in hats and men in sandals and women in Western pearl-snap shirts. Off to one side of the stage, a couple was swing-dancing, the man rag-dolling the girl around and then she'd snap back into step with him, just in time. It was quick and entertaining and Lander didn't even know Soleil was coming after him till she was standing there breathing tequila in his face.

"You aren't getting off that easy," she said. "Come on and dance. I can dance with two of you."

And Lander was going to say no, he meant to say no, but then he saw the proprietary look in his brother's eyes and decided what the hell. Like a dog in a manger: ain't going to eat

hay, ain't going to let nobody else eat hay, either. He tried to remember where he knew the joke from and then he was out on
the dance floor, doing the white-man dance next to his brother
while Soleil did her stripper moves. She had a nice big ass and
she knew how to shake it. She seemed like a nice-enough rich
girl and Lander wondered where she had gotten the hooker
clothes and the hooker moves. People were watching. She had
that go-anywhere, do-anything alcoholic burn in her eyes and
she kept shouting "Woo!"

Somewhere in here was when the guy in the black Resistol
started poking in.

He was just another man in the crowd, a drunk gent in
Western clothes, thirty or thirty-five, with an older, seamed
and dark-tanned face. The second or third time he came
through their little group was when Lander noticed him, and
thought that he looked like a cleaned-up guy from a road
crew and also that he looked like a man who might like to
fight. He had leather skin and deep angry lines around his
eyes. Lander looked around and wondered if these others—
there were several others who looked like him, sun-dried and
sun-baked—wondered if there was a crew of them to go along
with the man in the black hat. He had a little slurve in his
movements, a little drunken wobble on his high boots, and he
orbited around Soleil like a bug around a light.

It didn't take her long to notice. Maybe he was tall enough.
He wore brand-new Wranglers that looked like they had been
sprayed on. She circled back toward him and he performed a
little roosterish bob and weave. It was like watching a fucking

nature show, Lander decided, predator and prey—though it wasn't clear at this point in the dance which one of them was which. He had the home advantage but she looked like she might know a trick or two herself. First she was dancing with Tim, then with the two of them, then with the three of them, then with the man in the black hat alone. It was deftly done, by each of them. When the song ended, they glided toward the bar for another shot, his hand on her tattoo.

"We've got to get her out of here," said Tim.

"Why? She looks like she can take care of herself."

"You think her parents are going to like it?"

"You sure you don't have a little motive of your own?" Lander asked. "Besides, her parents have had plenty of practice by now, getting used to shit like this. That's my bet, anyway."

"Dad needs this," Tim said, his face suddenly up in Lander's face, right inside his personal space. Lander fought an urge to punch him away but Tim was intent. "Dad is fucking broke. What kind of a chance do you think he'd have with those two?"

"The parents?"

Tim nodded.

"About the same," Lander said. "Those two aren't buying shit. They're just along for the ride."

"What makes you say that?"

"Just a hunch."

"Your well-known hunches," Tim said. "They always work out so great."

"Look," Lander said. "You want me to go get your girlfriend, I'll go fetch her out of there, fine with me. Just get out of my face, Tim."

"I'm going with you."

"No, you're not. Sit your ass down."

"You can't tell me what to do."

"We'll settle this later, Tim. You want to fight, we can fight sometime when it won't put you in the hospital. Meanwhile, sit your ass down."

A moment, in which Tim was ready to punch him, almost did, finally didn't. They had been punching each other for eighteen years. Sooner or later they would have to quit. Maybe that time had come.

Tim looked from Lander to the door to the bar and back to Lander. "I'll wait here," Tim said.

"Good boy," Lander said. "Right back."

But turning from his brother to the circle of dark-faced men at the bar, circled around Soleil, he realized that he had no clear idea of what would happen next and no desire at all to do this. The band played "Don't Take Your Guns to Town" and Lander slowly walked toward the bar. The men—there were three or four of them—were clearly part of the same crew, highway workers or roofers, out in the sun, young men and middle-aged men who wore old men's skin. Soleil was standing in the middle, up against the bar, with her head thrown back and laughing and the original cowboy, the one in the black hat, was pretending to laugh with her and checking out her tits. Nothing wrong with that, Lander thought. He was just as guilty himself. The bartender, a solid tanklike woman in her fifties, set a beer down on the bar, took a twenty and went to make change. One of the friends noticed Lander walking up to them and then they shouldered one another and they all watched him.

"Come on, Soleil," Lander said. "We've got to get running."

"Now?"

"Now," Lander said.

"I don't want to go now," Soleil said.

"I can give her a ride," said the man in the black hat. He was leaning back against the bar now, with a bottle of beer in one hand, and he looked down at Lander from the height of his boots and he smiled in an unkind way. He said, "Be on your merry way."

"I don't think her mom and dad would appreciate that," Lander said.

"Who gives a fuck about my mom and dad?" said Soleil.

"You are a thumb-sucking nincompoop," Lander told her. "Just get in the car and let's go."

"What did you call her?" said the man in the black hat.

"Come on, let's go," Lander said, and took Soleil's wrist with his hand.

"*No*," she said, and they all looked down at where he had hold of her. The leathery man in the black Resistol looked back up, smiled into Lander's eyes, set his bottle of Coors Light back onto the bar with unhurried care and in one motion coldcocked Lander into the middle of the dance floor.

The punch hit Lander as a surprise and an immediate on-rush of pain. Everything went kind of swimmy and vague. He had a strong urge to get to his feet and punch the leathery man back, but he did not have the wherewithal to do so. Somewhere along the line he had let go of the girl. He looked up from the floor, expecting to be kicked. This man, whoever he was, had been in a bar fight before, and he would not be interested in ending it fairly or in a sportsmanlike manner. Lander knew that he had made a serious mistake in entangling himself in this and felt that he was about to pay the price for this mistake.

He looked up, expecting to be kicked, and what he saw was his brother wading in through the crowd, heading for the girl and the black-hatted cowboy, who was moving toward the dance floor against the wishes of the girl, who was screaming in a kind of a strange slow-motion way while the little Christmas lights twinkled and twirled behind her head. Lander had the dreamlike feeling of watching a thing unfold and being unable to move, unable to stop it. He felt like he could move if only he could get his brain to tell his body what to do but it was all lost in confusion.

He watched from the floor as Tim advanced on the man in the black hat, who stood coiled and ready. When Tim came within range, without preamble, he knocked him onto the dance floor, too. Tim landed unconscious with his eyes open.

In a moment, a few seconds, Tim started to puke blood.

The girl screamed. The cowboy stood there puzzled and angry, as if they had played a trick on him.

Lander got to his feet. He was suddenly better, suddenly clear-headed. The nearest emergency room would be in Kalispell.

"The door," he said.

"What?" said the girl.

"Get the door," he said, and lifted his brother from the floor, so light in his arms that he felt like a child, blood smearing both their shirts. The girl held the door and then suddenly she seemed to know what to do, too: she went to the pickup and flung the passenger door as far open as it would go, then got in, sat with her arms open as Lander passed his brother to her in the truck, cradling him in her arms. They folded him in and then Lander gently closed the door on them and then they were out of the parking lot in a shower of gravel.

"He's breathing," said the girl. "He's breathing fine."

Lander thought to answer for a moment but he was going a hundred by then and it was a bitch to keep the old truck on the road. It bucked and swayed like the derelict it was, onto the shoulder and then back across the center line, headlights raking the trees.

"Don't kill us," said the girl.

"I'm not going to kill us," Lander said. He knew the road like he knew his name, backwards and forwards, knew when to slow and when to speed. The lake glimmered in and out of the trees on his left, shining in the moonlight, restless. Low clouds shined over the surface of the water and it was like driving through a dark dream and at one point Lander was overcome with unreality, as if he would soon wake up sweating, with his feet burst through the bottom of the sheets.

Then he nearly put them in the lake, sliding through a turn he had forgotten. Then he slowed. Driving around Bigfork, stuck momentarily at a light, he saw the girl's hand gripped hard around the window crank, like that would save her. He peeled into the other lane, ran the red light and accelerated for Kalispell.

"The mint," said Tim. At least that's what it sounded like he said, low and indistinct.

"What's that?" asked the girl.

"Taking it to the mint," Tim said.

For whatever reason, this scared Lander worse than any of the rest of it and he drove with concentrated speed across the flat hayfields at the head of the lake, making enemies out of the other traffic as he swerved around them and passed with abandon, honking the horn of the old pickup, gunning the loud 283 under the hood. The lights of Kalispell were upon them and then streaking past. "Call 911," Lander said. "Tell them we're coming. Kalispell emergency room."

"Sure," said the girl. "What's the number?"

This hung in the air between them for a moment and then they both cracked up. This was the single stupidest thing anybody had ever said and he couldn't stop laughing at it and she couldn't, either. All the fear came out as laughter and they laughed at this all through Kalispell and were still laughing all the way to the canopy over the emergency room entrance, where they stopped.

"Open the door," he said, and Soleil did, and Lander came around the hood of the car and took his brother and carried him in his arms—so light since the accident! like carrying a child—into the emergency room, where the two or three people inside fell into a hush.

Lander looked down and saw the blood on his shirt, him and his brother both.

The lull gave way to quick activity and soon Tim was on a gurney and gone, back into the inner reaches of the hospital, without explanation or delay. Lander's part was done and only then did he realize that his mouth was dry and his hands were shaking. He went out to move the truck and outside the moon was flying through scraps and tatters of cloud, a werewolf kind of night but warm. Somewhere down at the lake, not far from here, people were sitting out on the dock and watching the stars come out, enjoying the quiet, the little lake-waves against the pilings of the dock. Somewhere people thought they were safe.

* * *

A n hour later, the doctor came out of the back and scanned the waiting room, looking for Lander. "Are you family?" he asked, and Lander nodded. "Come on back."

Something deadly in his tone, his eyes, and Lander followed him back expecting the worst. When he got into the curtained-off back, though, there was Tim sitting up in bed and smiling weakly.

"Hey," Tim said.

"Hey, Dumas," said Lander.

"Your brother has an ulcer," said the doctor. "I don't know how they missed it in the nursing home. I don't know what he was doing in the nursing home in the first place."

"I didn't really have anywhere else to go," Tim said.

Lander looked at him. He said, "You could have stayed with Mom."

"She's been kind of depressed this summer."

"Or me."

"Really?" Tim said. "I'll keep that in mind for next time. I don't know if you noticed, but I was a little pissed at you."

The doctor broke in halfway through. He said, "I just want to keep him here overnight, keep an eye on him. You can come and get him in the morning, though. I'm pretty sure he's all right."

Lander asked Tim, "Is that OK with you?"

"What are we going to do?" Tim asked. "Fight our way out of here?"

"I've had enough of that for one night."

"Me, too," Tim said. "I'll see you in the morning."

"Right you are," said Lander; took his brother's hand in his own, like a girl would, and held it to his chest. He said, "I'm fairly glad you're alive."

"Me, too," Tim said.

Then it was over, and Lander was out under the sky again, walking out toward the truck. Soleil, who had been sulking or sobbing in the corner of the waiting room all by herself, trailed a few feet behind him. He didn't know, until he got outside, how much he hated the air of the hospital, not just the scent of shit and rubbing alcohol but the contaminated lethal air itself. He didn't want it in his lungs.

"You didn't have to do that," Soleil said.

Lander didn't answer, just got into his side of the truck, unlocked her door for her, rolled down the window and started the engine. The cab still smelled a little like blood. If nothing else this summer, he wanted to get the smell of blood off him. He looked down at his stained shirt and knew it wouldn't happen tonight.

"None of this had to happen," said Soleil, as they stood at a stoplight in downtown Kalispell. It wasn't late but the streets were deserted, as if it were winter.

"Sure it did," said Lander.

"You could have just left me there," she said.

"I could have. I *would* have. But Tim wasn't going to."

"Why not?" she asked. "Seriously, I would have been fine."

"You would have been," Lander said, and wondered for a moment how much of an explanation he really owed her. But he felt like it. He said, "You would have been fucked, flustered and far from home, and that would have been fine with me. It was Tim that didn't want to leave you there. He had some dumbass idea that your folks were interested in a house up here. I told him you were just along for the ride, stringing my dad along, but he didn't believe me. I knew all the time."

"They might have," said Soleil.

"They might have," Lander said. "What's that?"

"Well, they might have."

"You're just a whole family of liars and whores, aren't you?"

Lander asked. This shut her up, and they drove in silence out of sleeping Kalispell, out into the hayfields and broken moonlight. Lander was suddenly exhausted, easy in his seat. He felt like this night had been going forever, days and nights all compressed into one, event piled on top of event and more to come. He would have to explain where his brother was when he got back. Just the thought of this sent the copper-penny taste into his mouth again and this time he recognized it as fear. Nobody would hit him or sue him or even talk badly to him. They just wouldn't want anything to do with him anymore.

"I do have some good points," Soleil said after a few miles.

"Like what?"

"I give a wicked blow job," she said. "Also I've been told that I'm a very good traveling companion. I'm always interested to see new things."

Lander laughed and shook his head. He said, "Those are important things to know about yourself, I guess."

"I'm sorry about tonight," she said.

"That's all right."

"No, I mean it. He's going to be OK, isn't he?"

"I expect he will," Lander said.

"I just get so cooped up," Soleil said. "I don't hate my parents or anything but after three days in the car with them, you know, I could scream. Then I get a chance to get away from them and then just run with it a little, I don't know . . . sometimes things just get out of hand."

"I can see that."

"I never mean for anybody to get hurt," she said, touching

Lander's thigh through the leg of his jeans. "It just happens that way sometimes."

The touch went through him like a solid poke to the funny bone, a sudden galvanic response on the part of his whole body, which reorganized itself around her touch. She seemed to have said everything she meant to and Lander didn't want to start anything new. He knew for certain that he would fuck this up somehow but he didn't want to just yet. He wanted her to leave her hand there, which she did. At the light in Bigfork—how long ago had they been there before? it felt like days—he pressed his own hand down along the top of hers, and Soleil gave him a thrilling little squeeze.

She took her hand away as they pulled into the drive of the marina. The *Lucky Me* was not at the dock. A fifty-foot hole in the line of boats where his father's boat was supposed to be.

"Where are they?" asked Soleil.

"Maybe they're up in the condo," Lander said.

"What did they do with the boat?"

This was not a question with an answer and Lander left it alone. He parked the truck and they went inside to investigate, the same odd sensation of no time and no air as before. In the artificial light and flocked wallpaper was the smell of death. The dried blood flaked and fell from his shirt. He checked his watch and it was not yet one o'clock in the morning, which was not possible. It felt like the day after tomorrow.

Nobody home in the condo, either.

Lander went into the back bedroom to change his shirt. All the laundry he had brought with him was worn but he found a black T-shirt that wasn't too bad. When he came out, Soleil was standing on the little concrete balcony, looking out over the lake. Lander was tired, deep-tired, but he didn't want to sleep just yet. He would have to solve the problem of the girl anyway, before he slept. He went to the refrigerator, which had magically refilled itself and was now full of beer, got one for himself and one for the girl and brought them out onto the balcony.

"Look," she said, and pointed out over the water.

Lander couldn't see a thing at first, just the lake, shimmering and shining in the moonlight as the clouds shifted, casting long blue shadows over the water. Then he saw it, a pale shape in the water, silent and drifting: the boat.

And there was Jen, out on the dock. Where had she been before?

Hello, she called through cupped hands, and Lander heard his father's answering voice, *Hello!*

What's wrong? Jen called, and his father answered, *Out of gas!*

What do we do? asked Jen, and his father said, *Too late!*

Then they left off shouting. There was maybe nothing more to say. As his eyes cleared into the dark, Lander could see the big boat clearly, see that it was moving only slowly toward the shore. They must have almost made it home. He must have just underestimated the distance, his father, or else he had been taken with one of his fits of optimism. We'll probably make it, his father would have said to himself. It's probably OK. Lander thought wistfully of the Orpheum, of the quiet, event-free nights. The wind was pushing the boat toward shore, toward the gravel beach at the state park, and not into the dock, which was just as well. Soon he would be back at the library, back in the quiet and the cool. Dishing up huckleberry, espresso Heath Bar, double chocolate, rum.

"What do we do now?" asked Soleil.

"We wait," said Lander. "The wind will bring it on to shore."

"And what shall we do while we wait?" asked Soleil, turning her back to the emergency so she could face him. Nobody knew they were there. Nobody would be paying the slightest attention.

"You are the craziest of them all," said Lander.

"Kiss me, kiss me, kiss me," said Soleil; and he did, he did, he did.

In the Burn

EDDIE'S SOCCER CAMP IS RUNNING LATE.
Nancy and I watch from the front seat of her Crown Vic,
smoking cigarettes and chewing Red Vines. It's a fall day,
beautiful, and the trees that line the playing field are red and
yellow and bright. A low slant of sunlight turns the windshield
half opaque with bug death and dried-up raindrops.

"I think he's doing better," I tell Nancy.

"Look at him," Nancy says. "He's in another universe."

Nancy shakes another cigarette out of her pack while I try
to think of some way to disagree with her. Eddie is definitely
her kid and she definitely loves him but she's hard on him
sometimes. Like now: he's out there with all the other boys in
their shin guards and uniforms and when the ball comes his
way, he'll kick it if it's in front of him. He runs up and down
the field like all the rest of them. But Eddie always seems kind

of surprised to see the ball when it shows up. He trails a little bit behind the action most of the time. Once in a while he looks like he's singing to himself.

"Ten kids out there playing soccer," Nancy says, "and one kid pretending to play soccer. My kid."

She exhales in a fifties-movie kind of way, almost a sigh. I reach in the back, get a beer out of the cooler. I've been fighting fires all summer and at this point I'm seriously recreating. Two showers a day, ice cream for breakfast. This is usually the best time of year: after I get off the fire line, and before I run out of money.

"Cut him some slack," I tell her. "He's only ten."

"Eleven," Nancy says.

"He'll pick it up."

"He won't," she says. "You know Jack."

Jack is her ex-husband, Eddie's father, not a successful human being.

"There's been some time and experiences that went into making Jack what he is," I tell her.

"He was like that before."

"I didn't know there was a before."

The other parents are on the sideline whooping it up, cheering for their kids, yelling at the coach or pulling him aside for a quiet talk. A couple of times I'd gone with Eddie, just the two of us, while Nancy was working—she's a swing-shift OR nurse at the hospital—and I'd stood on the sideline with the other parents but Nancy won't do it. She says she's tired of the dirty looks and she's got a point. These parents want to win,

win, win. When Eddie spaces out and misses a shot, they look at you.

"I need to find a way to make some money," Nancy says. "I need to get out of town for a while."

It's true she looks tired, more than she used to.

"I've got money," I tell her. "I've got a bunch of money. Let's go to Mexico. We could last out the winter down there, easily."

This is the way things have been between us since I got back: she shakes her head then takes a hit off her cigarette then looks at me like I'm an idiot. Three years ago, when I met her, she looked so much younger than she was. I was surprised to find out she was thirty-two. Three years ago, she used to pay attention to my little plans, she was always ready to go: Mexico, Thailand, anywhere. We were going to go back to North Carolina the other year, so I could show her where I came from, the beach and the tobacco fields and the Blue Ridge. But we never quite went anywhere.

"What then?" she says. "What do we do when we get back?"

I can't stand to see her so sarcastic and mean like this, though I know I deserve it. We could have gone to Thailand after fire season last year. I had the money. She had the vacation time.

"I'm going to go back to school," I tell her. "Finish up and get my teaching certificate. I told you."

"So you say."

"What does that mean?"

"You told me the same thing last year. Are you in school now?"

"I've been working."

She shakes her head again, this time sad instead of angry, and she takes my beer out of my hand and drinks from it. I take her cigarette from between her fingers and take a hit off it but I still can't smoke. Two months of breathing forest fire and now it feels like I've got gravel in my lungs.

"Plus I've got that application in for the disability," I tell her. "I'd lose that if I went back to school this fall."

"I slept with Jack again," she says.

I am not expecting this. It's like a bee or something buzzing around my ear and I shake my head to get rid of it but it won't go away. She slept with Jack.

"Why?" I ask her.

"I don't know," she says. "He wanted me to."

"No," I say. "Why'd you tell me?"

"I don't know," she says. She waves her cigarette at me as if her cigarette will tell me. She stares straight ahead out the windshield, out into the hard afternoon light. The boys are running, the parents are yelling, the leaves are turning.

Down deep under the earth, the plates are moving, the continents are shifting, so slowly we don't even feel it. All we can do is ride it. It's just a feeling I have, something I know. Nancy's crying now, but in that private way that doesn't mean me any good. It's her suffering, her tears. It seems to me that I ought to be mad and that I'm not. I just have this feeling that

I'm floating above this whole scene and it's not really happening to me. I'm trying to feel it, trying to make myself remember that I was out on the fire line breathing smoke while she was fucking him between nice clean sheets. A man would be angry, thinking about this. A man ought to be angry.

But I see it from like a million miles away and it's like somebody else. Watching Nancy cry.

"You didn't have to tell me."

"I did." Now she's using her nurse voice. It's the way she talks to her patients, the way she gets them to do things for her, but not because she wants them to. It's for their own good.

Another minute of staring out the window, breathing, smoking. The smoke in the car is getting to me and I open the window and the cool fall air comes pouring in, air that feels like it's full of the sunlight that runs through it. It's like medicine to me, like a cold beer on a hot afternoon: clear light and clean air.

"We're not going anywhere, you and me," she says. "We're just more of the same when we're together. And I want out, Richard. I'm tired of not having any money, tired of taking care of Eddie by myself. I want somebody to take care of me, at least a little."

"I was just working," I tell her. "I was out making money. What's wrong with that?"

"I want a house," she says.

"I'll buy you a house," I tell her.

"No, you won't."

And Nancy sounds so blue when she says this. I touch her

arm, the soft skin at the inside of her wrist, and I bring her arm toward me and I kiss her palm, the inside of her wrist, the soft place. The plates are moving under us, the continents and seas.

When we look up, Eddie's staring at us through the passenger-side window where I'm sitting.

"Hey buddy-boy," I tell him. "You looked pretty good out there."

"What were you two talking about?" he asks.

"I've got to get to work," Nancy says.

Eddie looks hurt—he's being told to shut up and he knows it—but he doesn't say anything, just climbs into the back seat of Nancy's big Crown Vic and lies down.

"I'm tired," he says. "Can we go to the Dairy Queen?"

Nancy starts to shake her head to say no, but I break in.

"After we drop your mom at work," I tell him.

Nancy gives me a dirty look but fuck her. I'm not breaking up with Eddie. Eddie's not telling me to get lost.

"I hate soccer," Eddie says.

"Don't start," says Nancy. "There's only three more weeks to go."

"But I don't like it," Eddie says. "I don't like it and I'm no good at it and what's the point?"

"I thought you looked OK out there today," I tell him—and both mother and child give me a dirty look at this.

Nancy and I sit at opposite ends of the front seat, which is a good ways apart in this car. I don't even know what I'm supposed to be feeling. When we drop her at the hospital Nancy gives me a quick peck on the cheek, then looks back over at Eddie. Which means what? Don't tell Eddie, is what it means. All this is too confusing for me. I don't want to hurt his feelings. But I don't want him to just wake up some morning—tomorrow morning, the day after—and find me gone.

"You be good," Nancy says, and closes the door. It isn't clear whether she means me or Eddie or both. When she disappears inside the revolving door, Eddie slides over the seat back and up front next to me, which Nancy normally won't let him.

"Dude," Eddie says.

"Where to?" I ask him.

"Dairy Queen, definitely," he says. "What's up with her?"

"Nothing, dude."

"The Momster," Eddie says. "The Momster's on a rampage."

It isn't exactly clear whether he's talking to me or just thinking out loud; whether he means what he says or whether he's just saying it to see what it sounds like. Eddie is that kind of a child.

Four o'clock and the streets are all clean with light, kids going home from school or just hanging around. It's warm but you can tell it won't be soon.

"Double Blizzard," Eddie says. "Heath Bar and cookie dough."

"That'll be extra," says the girl in the cage.

Eddie looks at me and I shrug.

"No problem," Eddie says. "He's paying."

"And what for you?"

"Nothing for me," I tell her.

I'll land on my own two feet, I know it. I was all alone and lonely and sexually deprived when I met her. I can do it again. But just the thought of my little apartment with my little clothes in it sends a willie down my back. One more night of TV, one more night of wondering where I'm supposed to be in this world.

"What do you want to do?" I ask Eddie.

A double Blizzard, it turns out, is a couple of pounds of stuff, and Eddie sits on top of the picnic table with his legs dangling and works at it with a spoon while he thinks. He's got short hair but he's got this one long braid, about as thick as a pencil and halfway down his back. He's wearing soccer shorts and a team shirt, which don't look at all right on him, and he has already ditched the shin guards and tall socks. Even with the whole rig on, he doesn't look like a little English boy, like he's supposed to. He looks captured and nervous, like those old Indian pictures where they're in a suit and you can't tell if they're being made fun of.

"Dude," he says. "Let's go ride that Suzuki."

He says it cool and casual, looking into his Blizzard. He says it about once a week. But this time I surprise him.

"Sure," I tell him. "Let's go."

He stares at me, blinking, trying to see if I'm lying.

"Drink up," I tell him. "Eat up, whatever, let's go."

"The Momster will not like this."

"She said it was all right," I tell him; and then, when he looks up at me, blinking, I tell him: "That's what I thought I heard her say, anyway."

"Ah," says Eddie.

He thinks for a second.

"Dude," he says.

*   *   *

A n hour later we're riding way above the valley, out on the fire road where I was working a month ago, way past the houses we saved, deep in the burn. Eddie's wearing every piece of winter clothing he owns and I'm the one who's freezing. But Eddie's having a good time and I'm not going to stop. I can hear him singing to himself behind me. I can feel him holding on.

The burn flashes by in patches of sunlight and shade, in green and black and shades of gray. The sunlight's blinding when it comes full tilt. I have to slow, to clear my head and guess where the road goes, lost in the dazzle. The road is ragged and scarred, bare dirt and dozer tracks and patches of mud, everything dirty, the green leaves trampled down into the dirt, washed with mud. Where there are any green leaves, one side of the road. I get to a little clearing where you can see out over the burn and I stop the bike and the quiet rushes in, all around us.

"This is where we started the backfire," I tell Eddie. "The fire came up over that ridge over there and started to burn down toward us. We just started on this road, right here, and burned it right back to the fire, stopped it dead."

Eddie doesn't say anything, just takes his helmet off and looks around. He's a little freaked out, I guess. Or maybe I'm just used to it: the smell of the smoke, the taste of smoke and creosote in the back of my throat. When the wind blows, we can hear branches cracking off and falling in the burned hills in front of us. Once in a while, a whole burned tree will fall, or two. It's a big sound.

"Dude," Eddie says.

"It's big, isn't it?"

"It looks like an army went here," Eddie says. "It looks like a war."

"It's closer than you think," I tell him. "We had five hundred soldiers from Georgia out here, the week things started blowing up."

Tripping over their own dicks. But I don't say that to Eddie.

"It looks just dead out there," Eddie says.

"You'd be surprised," I tell him. "Come back in a year or two, when it's all greened up, you'll find a lot of stuff in here. Animals and stuff, berries. The elk really like it."

"You're right," Eddie says. "I'd be surprised."

We stand there quiet for a moment, listening to the wind running through the black trees, breathing ash and smoke. Something big happened here, something out of control, you can feel it. I'm wondering how much of this Eddie will remember when he's grown up. Myself at ten or eleven, I remember only in little flashes and pictures and sometimes the smell of a certain kind of pine tree. They don't have the white pines out west that we had in North Carolina but there's a kind of sugar pine that smells almost the same, needles drying in the afternoon sun. Maybe when Eddie's grown up, he'll smell a campfire and remember this.

"I'm going to make a world just like this," Eddie says.

"Say what?"

"In Warcraft Three," he explains to the retarded boyfriend. "This would be k-e-w-l, get like the orcs coming up out of the valley. Is that on fire?"

I look down and there's smoke coming out of a matchstick pile of downed trees.

"It'll burn till the snow comes," I tell him. "Nothing's going to put the fire all the way out. But there's nothing to worry about. There's nothing much left to burn."

"There's a dog down there," Eddie says.

I look way down the hill and I don't see anything, nothing moving, just the black snags and the gray dust blowing along the black ground. Then I see what he's talking about: a little gray spot moving slowly through the burn, unhurried.

"That's like a skunk or a raccoon or something," I tell Eddie. "It's too little to be a dog."

"It's a little dog," Eddie says.

"I need glasses."

"It is."

I wish he wasn't but Eddie's right: it's a dog. Fuck.

"What's he doing down there?" I say.

"Not much," Eddie says. "Looking for his home."

"That's the one," I tell him. "That's the dog."

"Which?"

"Those three houses that burned?" I tell him. "Down in O'Brien Creek? All of them got all their stuff out except for the one family, they had everything loaded up to go. But the dog jumped out and went running back, right when they were leaving. It was in the papers."

"They didn't go back for it?"

Eddie looks hurt and puzzled and angry and I have forgotten that he is still at least part-child. In Eddie's world, no one would ever leave their dog behind, no one would ever say forget it, it's just a dog. In Eddie's world, people race back into burning buildings, they turn over wrecked cars, so that their dog will live. They don't just walk away. They couldn't.

"The fire crew wouldn't let them," I tell Eddie. "The fire was already up and over the hill."

"They could have just gone back for it."

They could have but they didn't, is the truth. But Eddie's never seen that wall of fire coming after you, never heard the noise it makes.

"I'll go get the dog and we can give it back to them," I tell Eddie. "You wait up here."

He looks at the sky and then he looks at my face. He doesn't want to.

"There's hot spots, still," I tell him. "Step on one of those in your sneakers and you'll burn yourself. I'm not kidding."

"I'll be careful," Eddie says.

I look at him sideways—the one thing Eddie's never been is careful—but he wants to come. And I'm not going to tell him he can't.

And besides, as we start down the hill I start to think that I want him to see me do this. I want to be somebody's hero, at least for a day. We might even make the papers, the dog rescuers. Eddie's sticking close behind me and I can hear him humming, singing a little to himself, which is what he does when he's happy; and all at once I feel something collapse inside me, some little dam that was holding back the feeling, and I know all at once how much I could do for him, how much he is going to miss me and how much I am going to miss him.

"Cut it out," I tell him.

"What?"

"The singing," I tell him. "Cut it out."

"I didn't even know I was," he says, and he stops, which makes me feel worse. Why can't he be happy? Why can't one of us?

In a minute he starts again, which makes me feel worse again, but this time I don't make him stop.

The way down is rocky and loose, which is good from the standpoint of not being on fire. I fall on my ass a couple of times but Eddie never slips. The fire is all around us, not quite out, smoldering in the black branches and standing snags. The smell is worse here, off the road, and it just feels dangerous. He shouldn't be here, Eddie shouldn't. Nancy would sue if she knew about it.

And then, halfway down, we lose the dog. That is, I'm looking at my feet and the rock in front of me, trying to pick a way down, and when I look up again the dog is gone.

"You see him?" I ask Eddie.

"Who?" he says, and I know right away that he has been spacing out, singing his little happy song.

"The dog," I say.

"He's down here somewhere," Eddie says. "We'll find him, don't worry."

"I'm not worried," I say, although I ought to be. We've got no business down here, and night is not far off. The sun is already down behind one of the burned hills and everything is black or gray, no color, no water, nothing but ash and smoke.

When we get to where we saw the dog, nothing.

"Where'd he go?" I ask Eddie.

"There," he says. "He's over there."

"Did you see him?"

"No, I—never mind," Eddie says, embarrassed. "Really, he's over there."

He points, and I see a little path through the black trees and ashes and I follow it, wondering what just happened. What did Eddie know? Plus the dark is creeping in around us. I am going to freeze my ass off on the ride home, at a minimum.

And there in front of me is the dog.

It stands there staring back at me, somebody's little fluff-ball once, a dog a little bigger than a cat. The fur is long and matted and stained with ash and the little eyes are wide and frightened. A long still moment in which I watch the dog and the dog watches me.

Then I reach my hand out toward the dog and the thing lunges toward me and bites my hand, hard.

"You little fuck," I say, and try to wrench my hand away but the dog holds on, holds on so hard that I actually pick it up by the grip on my hand and shake the thing off in midair. The air hits the flap of skin that the dog tore away and the pain comes up hot and quick. The dog scampers back toward the edge of the little clearing. It still hasn't barked, hasn't made a sound. I take my handkerchief from my back pocket and wrap it around my hand. I still don't want to look at what the bite did. I don't want to know.

"Hey, sport," Eddie says. "Hey, buddy."

He's on his knees in front of me, talking to the dog. He knows I'll kick it if I get the chance. It's like I'm not even there, the way he's talking to the dog, so calm and slow; like none of this is there, not me, not the smoke, the black trees and the gathering dark. Eddie just kneels there, talking slow and soft about nothing, saying, Hey champ, hey sport, hey dog, how are you?

I can feel it. It's working.

It's working on me, too, the way I just let the anger drop away, and the fear, the gathering dark and my bleeding, torn hand and the smoke and ash around us. Eddie knows something, something I don't.

After a minute the dog just walks over to Eddie and rests its head on his lap and rolls over, belly up.

"It's a girl, isn't it?" Eddie says.

"It's a girl, definitely."

"She's so tired," Eddie says. And he's right, you can see it, it's like she gives up all at once, open and vulnerable. It's all right if we take her, all right if we kill her. She's putting herself in Eddie's hands. She's wide open. You can feel how scared and tired she has been, walking alone through the burn, looking for a house that was no longer there, a family, an owner, somebody.

"Let's go," I tell Eddie. "It's getting dark."

"One minute," he says. He needs that minute to calm her down, I guess. Something. I really have no idea what he's doing or how he does it but he's doing it. He takes his outer jacket off—he's wearing about three of them—and takes the sweater underneath and wraps the little dog in it, then bundles both of them up in his jacket again. The little dog head peers out of the zipper, just under his chin.

"OK," he says. "Let's go."

Eddie leads the way up the hill, with me behind to catch him if he falls, but he doesn't need me. I don't even realize how dark it's gotten till I fire up the bike and see the headlight stab out into the trees. Eddie clambers on behind, the little dog still tucked in his jacket. I imagine that I can feel her heartbeat through my back, although I know it isn't so.

The ride back to town is so cold I can't even feel my hand anymore, cold and colder still, the wind whipping at my face and Eddie holding tight behind. I stop at the fire headquarters out at the Fort. I figure somebody will be glad to see this dog. Maybe we'll get our picture in the paper.

But when we get to the fire center, there's nobody around.

A month ago, this looked like war, with helicopters buzzing in and out and backcountry fire trucks and a tent city of firefighters out back. Now it's like somebody cut the power. I shut the bike down and we go looking for somebody, anybody. It's strange, it was such a big deal, such an effort, such a feeling that it mattered, that lives and homes and even cities were at stake, and now it's over. We have to try three doors before we find one that isn't locked.

Inside a duty officer sits at a table with a phone and a computer, which he's playing solitaire on.

"We found the dog," Eddie says. "The dog that was missing."

He unzips his jacket and takes the dog and sets it on the floor. In the overhead lights, I can see that it once was white, that its eyes are red, that its paws are hurt, probably burned.

"Where'd you find that?" asks the duty officer.

"Up in the Black Mountain burn," I tell him. "I was just showing him—I was on that fire."

"Were you?" says the duty officer, but he's not interested in me. He comes around the desk and hunches down and looks the dog in the eye.

"Whose little dog are you?" he asks it. "And what the hell were you doing up on Black Mountain?"

"It's the dog that ran away," Eddie says.

The duty officer stays down for a minute, thinking, looking at the dog. Then straightens himself up again.

"I don't think so," he says. "That one was a Lab cross. Big dog. This isn't him. You might want to get that dog to a vet."

I can't see Eddie's face but I know the disappointment I'm feeling. Just for once I would like to do something right, to have it work out. That idiot my mom used to go out with. This could have been something real, something to remember.

But Eddie is not that kind of a kid. He's grinning when he turns toward me.

"Dude," he says. "I get to keep it!"

"You might want to talk to your mother about that."

Eddie lifts his little finger toward me and wiggles it in the air. "Wrapped around my finger," he says. "I've got her right where I want her."

"We'll see," I tell him. "It's up to you and her."

"Well," the duty officer says. "Back to work."

"Anything going on?"

"Just cleanup," he says. "That rain last week put everything down pretty good. Some rehab, you know."

Eddie scoops the dog up and puts her back in his jacket. She goes to him eagerly, she licks his hand. I can feel the ooze and seep of blood where she bit me, and in that moment I feel that everyone in the world is inside and I am out alone; that everyone is warm and safe, that circle of love is closed and everyone else inside and me out in the dark. That's what I feel.

Nancy's waiting for us when we get back to her house. She comes out onto the porch to yell at me.

"Where the hell have you been?" she says.

"Aren't you supposed to be at work?" I ask her.

"I called and called and you weren't here," she says. "You weren't here and you weren't at your place. Where were you?"

She sees the bleeding hand then, and she's already seen the motorcycle. Quickly she turns to Eddie to see that he's all right and that's when she sees the dog.

"What the hell is that?" she says. "Where did that thing come from?"

"I'll be around back," Eddie says, and slips away through the side gate, leaving the two of us in the porch light. He never likes to hear us fight. For a moment I think Nancy's going after him but in the end she just shakes her head.

"What did you do to your hand?" she says.

"That thing bit me."

Her eyes open wide.

"It's not going to bite Eddie," I tell her. "Don't worry. He's got the touch."

"What does that mean?"

I explain then—about the motorcycle ride, about the burn, the little dog down the hill and Eddie's magic trick. Standing in the porch light I explain that I wanted Eddie to see the parts of me he never saw, the rush I got from the bike, the place where I worked and the kind of work I did. I can't see her face or anything—she's standing with her back to the light—so I don't know how Nancy is taking any of this, but I tell her that I'm going to miss her, that I'm going to miss Eddie, too. But I think it's time for me to go.

I still can't see her face, dark against the light. In a minute she's going to let me go. Instead she says, "No, stay. Stay the night anyway. I've got the night off now."

It won't do any good. None of this will stop. I can feel the plates and planets splitting apart, the ground giving way under my feet. And tomorrow we will only have to do this all again. But tonight I want to be inside, inside the lit rooms of Nancy's house, breathing the same breath as her and Eddie and the idiotic little dog.

"All right," I tell her. And let myself be led, up the short stairs and into the warmth of her house and into her bathroom, where she peels the bandanna off my hand. The cut doesn't look as big or bad as it feels.

"Let's have a look," she says. "Take your jacket off."

I do as she tells me, wait for her in the bathroom as she gathers a butterfly bandage, a bottle of peroxide, a roll of gauze and a roll of tape, as Nancy runs the warm water and then peers into my cut palm as if my fortune was there.

"This is going to hurt," she says.

They Were Expendable

AFTER YOU DIED CAME the year of watching television. Mornings were the *Today* show and Internet radio in my office, pure meaningless noise. Lunch in a Greek place that always had the Atlanta Braves if they were on. Evenings I spent in the wonderland of cable, seventy channels of nothing, baseball nothing, infomercial nothing, animal-documentary nothing, Letterman-Leno-Conan nothing.

I gravitated toward channel 54, the war-movie channel. Once it was more of an all-purpose old-movie channel, but that year it was all war movies, and above all the Big One, Doubleyou Doubleyou Two. Patton and I chased Rommel across North Africa, Admiral Yamamoto and I bombed Pearl Harbor in a daring daylight raid. I joined the Greatest Generation: a twelve-pack of Rainier and three hours of *Tora! Tora!*

Tora! Cliff Robertson and I swam ashore from the wreck of the *PT 109*.

And John Wayne and I said good-bye to Donna Reed, knowing that we would not see each other again in this life, in the Philippines or anywhere else. We did not fuss or cry. Each of us going to fight the Japanese in our own way. To *soldier on*.

Also—since I am confessing—I bought a sex video from the adult shop downtown. It had a black-haired trashy beauty on the cover but inside was a woman as blonde as you, which was a mistake. Her face was entirely different, and her breasts were enormous. But still sometimes, seeing the back of her head or the small of her back, a little movement she made with her hand, I thought of you. A moment in particular in one of the passages of narration between sex scenes, a moment in which she turns her face up into the light, just before her face came into full view, a glimpse of dirty blonde hair and a small ear and a glimpse of neck—I would freeze this frame sometimes because it seemed to me that you were in it.

And all our friends, you know, they did what friends are for: they invited me to ball games, to picnics, to dinner parties and hikes. I did what I could stand to do. I didn't hurt their feelings. Days in football season when all I wanted was to lie on the couch and watch the Lions, the Packers, the Vikings and the Saints—days that would have passed as easily as water through my fingers—instead I packed up my fanny pack with my binoculars and water bottle and chased Bruce and Nancy up mountain trails. I was not quite fat but getting there, with all the American beer and football. I was out of breath and usually getting rained on and really I couldn't tell Bruce or Nancy, but really I didn't give a shit about the scenic splendors of the Columbia Gorge. I just wanted to be home with my remote.

But home was the one place no one wanted me. They didn't understand—that home was the one place I could be without you, lost in the rainy Philippines, torpedoing the Japs.

Or maybe it was this: somehow it became my job to keep them from the things they shouldn't know. In Bruce and Nan's world, in Tom and Chris and Janet and Jenny's world, it was possible to console. These small necessary acts of friendship, these dinners and movies and dance performances (yes, I went to dance performances, several) were not enough but they were not *nothing*. I could not, without hurting their feelings, tell them that really they were making things worse for me, making me feel and think and talk.

And I did not wish to hurt their feelings. Here are the things I have learned: there is enough suffering in this world; there is no use for suffering; there is no making sense of things sometimes.

And so when Jenny called to ask if I wanted to go to the movies, when she actually came by the house to check (for they had gotten used to me hiding behind the answering machine), I could not say no. I had to help her believe in her ability to help.

She caught me in my sweat pants and T-shirt, eating Chinese food alone in the blue flickery glow of *Who Wants to Be a Millionaire*. "No, come," said Jenny. "Keep me company. It's some awful chick-flick comedy type of thing and Tom has to work tonight."

"He wouldn't go with you anyway," I told her.

"No, but you will," Jenny said. "I'm going to make you."

"Have an egg roll," I told her.

"Have you been smoking again?"

"Just a little."

"Hmmm," she said, and took the egg roll and nibbled at it, and as her eyes adjusted to the dark, she took a good long searching look at my coffee table: a bong, my college bong, sitting out in plain sight, along with a couple of empty beer cans, little white boxes of Szechuan pork and fried rice, a half-empty pack of Camel Lights and one of your flowery teacups full of ashes and butts.

"You're going to the movies," she said. "No question about it. Hurry! Chop chop!"

I forget what movie it was—it might have actually *been* *Sleepless in Seattle*—but I'll tell you what it was for me. It was sitting in the dark with a woman beside me, just the proximity and the smell of some sweet product, maybe it was perfume or maybe it was some skin thing or moisturizer, I never really figured out what was what even in all the time we had together. And then when you were gone I just took all that stuff and threw it in the Dumpster. But just the way a woman smells, and the occasional accidental touch of bare arm to bare arm. It was the longest movie.

And then afterward we went to the Virginia Café, which was close by and I could have been home watching *Sands of*

Iwo Jima, I know, I saw in the TV guide. I listened to Jenny complain about how much Tom was working. It was just the VC to her, the place we used to go before we all got so busy. I know she didn't know. But all the time I was thinking of that Happy Hour when I got drunk and told you I loved you and how that seemed to come as a surprise to you.

And then—this is the hard part, love—there was this girl, came into the bar out of the rain, all by herself, dressed in black, a friend of Jenny's. Her name is Eleanor.

She's nothing like you.

I don't know for certain that this was Jenny's doing— Eleanor and I won't talk about it—but you're right, it does seem a little odd that this friend of Jenny's was just coincidentally in this bar that Jenny had coincidentally dragged me into. She was your closest friend, I know. Maybe this will seem like betrayal and maybe it won't.

And it's true that I was angry at both of them at first. It was just too hard, you know? to be in a bar, to talk to a girl, to buy her a drink and another drink and ask her where she worked and where she went to college and how did she like Portland? It turns out she's *from* Portland. She plays drums in a band called Bastard Amber. She's a lot younger than you were, a lot younger than me, and she's got that whole punk awful-hair thing, generally black-to-blonde but sometimes with pink frosting or little beaded braids. It's kind of entertaining, actually, to see what she'll turn up with.

And she's big, did I tell you? She's a big girl. She's really nothing like you.

I don't even know if you would like her.

She has this little apartment, little but very nice and very clean with nice old wood furniture, not at all what you would expect from a girl with pink hair. No television but lots of books and records, which made me uncomfortable right away. Because I'm not like that, it's a game I never win, the last book I read was *Moneyball*, about the Oakland As, I really enjoyed it. And also, I like music just fine, but it's not a religion for me or anything. Eleanor, anytime you see her she's got headphones on, and loud enough to hear it across the room, that little chirp-chirp-chirp. You know me: I like dumb bands, I like to hop around like an idiot, turn it up loud and make a fool of myself. But Eleanor likes these serious bands, Sonic Youth, Throwing Muses. I don't know what to do with that.

But look: that night, after Jenny "remembered" she had an "appointment" really early the next morning and really really had to go—it was still only eleven o'clock—there were really only two ways to go: shake hands and say good night, or else run with it. And I just remember, I had this moment where I saw myself like somebody else would see me, sitting on the couch in my shorts and college sweatshirt watching Robert Mitchum, watching James Cagney, watching Robert Montgomery, and I just thought No. Enough.

And then I woke up on her couch the next morning. I woke up to the sound of the coffee grinder and a foul mouth and the rain in the bushes outside her window and an instant, blue-light headache. Eleanor came into the kitchen doorway and looked at me like something she had never seen before.

"I have to go to work," she said. Then, after a minute, as if she were coming to some kind of conclusion: "I feel vile."

"I feel worse."

"No," she said thoughtfully, "no, that isn't possible. Were we smoking cigarettes?"

"I was."

"And I said it was all right to smoke in here?"

"No, wait," I said. "You were, too."

"Jesus fucking Christ," she said, looking at the ashtray on the end table, the wineglass smeared with lipstick.

Just then the kettle started to whistle in the kitchen and she left me to tend to it. I rolled the open sleeping bag off my body. I was still clothed. I had no memory of anything but conversation the night before but I was also missing some time off the end of the evening, a gradual fade to black.

In the kitchen, Eleanor was pouring water through a coffee filter, and the smell of fresh coffee permeated my body. It would either cure me or kill me.

"You were so cute last night," she said. "You wanted to drive home."

"I did?"

"You don't remember?"

I shook my head.

She said, "There's an extra toothbrush in the drawer next to the sink," which I took as a hint. My face in the mirror, I thought, looked a little like Lon Chaney Jr. in the early stages of his conversion to the Wolf Man. The toothbrush was right where she said it would be, all in its neat little unopenable wrapper, which made me wonder what I was getting into. How often she did this, how much of a pro she was.

And then all at once I thought of you, I remembered you. And I felt this great sensation of betrayal, as if by forgetting you—by drinking and talking and carrying on as if you had never been in my life—I had let you disappear. Because I knew that in my heart was the last place in the world you lived. I saw your face, I felt your skin on the palms of my hands.

"What's wrong?" she asked, when I came into the kitchen again; and then she said, "Oh."

"It's nothing," I told her. "It's nothing with you."

"I know," she said. "I mean, I don't know. But you don't have to tell me."

"I mean . . ."

"Sshhh," she said, and handed me a hot cup of coffee. Then looked at me musingly for another long minute, asking my face some kind of question, then reached her own face up toward mine and kissed me, slowly, softly kissed me.

I did let myself be kissed.

Then she backed away and began to study me again.

"Eleanor," I said.

But she shushed me again. "No explanations," she said. "No talking, no expectations. I just was curious to see what that would feel like."

"And?"

Eleanor laughed. "I feel vile," she said.

And what? what happened in that moment? I touched it later, carried it around with me, felt the aftereffects of that kiss for a few days as if it had taken place just a minute before. The best I can say is that it was like a recognition, a sudden recognition that there was a person in there, live and warm in the cold world. It was very odd, really. I had no idea what had happened in that kitchen or what—if anything—was supposed to happen next. But I would be at work, or in my bed, or on a crowded, rainy sidewalk downtown, and the image of that moment would come to me, the kiss, the quizzical look, and when I remembered it I would stop for a minute, whatever I was doing, and laugh.

I can feel you getting ahead of me on this. You always knew my secrets before I knew them myself, which isn't hard—I stumble along blind. I try for this and I reach for that and when I finally figure out what's going on, I always find you there waiting for me. You know me always better than anyone.

But we didn't sleep together, not at first. We spent the next month getting drunk in each other's company, seriously drunk. I woke up on her couch twice more, once with a Monopoly piece—the little metal Scottie—clutched tightly in my hand.

Then it was time.

I don't know how we knew but it was time. Eleanor called me up at work, which she could do by then, and I heard it in her voice. It filled me with a kind of fear that I could feel in my body, a line we had to cross. I wanted to, she wanted to, in a strange way neither of us wanted to but we had to. It was time. I met her downtown and we had dinner at a restaurant you had never been to, I made sure of that. I wore clothes I had bought in the year after you had gone. Talking and talking,

talking about nothing, Eleanor and I had spent a month by then talking and drinking and laughing at each other's jokes but that night we couldn't seem to find it. We sat there pushing sushi around on our plates for a while and then it was time. We bought a bottle of good champagne and we went to Eleanor's apartment, where you have never been, where you will never be, except that night.

We undressed each other as decorously as adults unwrapping their birthday presents, attending to the decorations, taking their time. Her body was, at first, not beautiful to me. She was so unlike you, so big, and she carried herself in the light like she was ashamed of her body.

In the dark, though, she was strong and big and beautiful and she knew what she wanted.

It didn't happen.

And after we had failed, we sat on her sofa again and we tried to talk but we couldn't find any.

"I don't know," she finally said. "I'm going to have to think about this."

"I know."

"No, you don't," Eleanor said. "She's everywhere, all around you. It's like some kind of mist. Every time I think I see you, you disappear back into the mist."

"I'm sorry," I told her.

"There's nothing to be sorry for," she said. "It's nothing that you did or didn't do. Unless there's something you're not telling me."

We exchanged tight little laughter, nothing-funny laughter.

67

"I'm innocent," I said. "I'm innocent of *that*, anyway."

But, you know, it must have been something in the way I said it, something about the way I felt like I was making a joke about you—Eleanor saw you in my face, and drew away from me. Physically I felt her move her body away from me as if my touch repelled her.

"I'm sorry," I said again. "Maybe I should go."

"Maybe you should," she said.

Something spoiled about me, about my body, something rotted and wrong. That's what it felt like afterward, on my couch again, except that this time the noise would not work. The late-night racket of the television could not obscure the afterimage of her soft hand and then her mouth on my cock, the puzzlement and sorrow in her eyes. At least we had answered the question. At least we *knew*: my place was here, with you, and nowhere else in the world.

Suddenly it was easy, a kind of letting go. I drank till there was nothing more to drink and then I called in sick the next morning and went back to bed.

I didn't hear from her, didn't see her for the next two days.

On the evening of the third day she came by unannounced. I was on my couch, again, with a beer in my hand, again, and the remains of a pizza on the coffee table before me. After that first night, I wasn't going crazy drinking, but I was keeping up a steady flow, timing it (or trying to time it) so I could sleep at the end of the night. And I guess a couple of the empty cans were on the table, and cigarettes and so on. I had the lamps off, and the television filled the room with a blue flickery light like underwater.

The doorbell rang and I didn't want to answer it. I was all right; or if I wasn't exactly all right, I wasn't exactly present either. As close to nothing as I could get. That's what I wanted. But the blue light gave me away; the doorbell rang again.

Eleanor was standing in the porch light looking small and sad.

"Come in," I told her. "Sit down. Do you want anything to drink?"

"How much have you been drinking?"

"A little."

She looked at my face. "Give me something, then," she said. "Something to catch me up, like vodka or something. Do you have any vodka?"

She settled for Genever gin, a real back-of-the-liquor-cabinet special left over from some recipe or some party. I had drunk all the rest up. This was the first time she had been to the house and she moved through the dark hallways warily, as if she might be trapped there. I opened another beer and we sat together on the couch and I waited for the bad news. You could see the bad news in her face, even in the dim light of the TV.

"How have you been?" she asked.

"I'm all right," I said. "I've missed you."

"You didn't call."

"I didn't know if I was supposed to."

"No," she said. "Well . . ."

I could feel it coming, that next thing, and I didn't want to hear it. I didn't know I loved her until I felt her next to me, until I felt her leaving. I touched the soft skin of her arm, as lightly as I could. I didn't know if I loved her or not, didn't care if that was the right word or not, but I felt her leaving and I didn't want her to go.

I shut the television off and we sat together in the dark for a minute, with just the light from the kitchen shining down the hall. I couldn't see her face: a white blur in the half-light. Then I touched her breast through the fabric of her shirt.

"Don't," she said, and I put my hand down.

But then I kissed her, eyes closed, beautiful.

I felt her stiffen under my touch and then I felt her body relax beneath me and I knew what she was feeling: whatever, whatever happens next is whatever happens, it's all too difficult to figure out.

And then I was leading her through the dark hallways of our house and you were *there* and *there* and *there* and I took her anyway—down the hall to the back of our house and into our bedroom, yes and I stood and I undressed her in the same place, with the same sound of water in the leaves outside the open window, yes the sheets you bought, yes the comforter, yes the photograph on the wall you bought from the Saturday market was watching us as I undressed her and then I undressed and then we were on the bed—*our* bed—and with anger and something like despair I pushed inside her and all the time I thought of you.

And all the time I thought of you, I thought of you as I kissed the bare skin of her neck and kissed her breasts and Eleanor—give her credit—Eleanor was scared and wary and for a moment she may have been weeping, it was dark, I couldn't tell. It felt violent and wrong, what we were doing. It felt like blood, like breaking glass.

You were still there when we were done.

This is what I came to tell you, love: that life loves life. You were there but Eleanor was there beside you. She still is, you still are, the three of us in a tangle. I didn't mean to hurt you, I don't even know if you were watching or not, I'll never know. But life loves life.

That night we disentangled from the sheets and dressed partway and went back to our drinks in the living room, touching the whole time, like the other would disappear if we let go. There seemed to be nothing to say. The house seemed larger than it was, there in the half-dark. We sat for a while saying nothing, just touching.

Then it was all right to turn the light on, the one lamp beside the sofa, dim, and even in the light she was still there. We were together in the living room and it was all right.

"This place is a mess," she said, though she didn't seem to mind.

I shrugged. There was nothing to say.

Eleanor started to touch the objects on my coffee table, one by one: the bong was still there, the almost empty pizza box, the lighter, she touched each of them, either to make them real or to make them hers, I don't know which. She never let go of me with her other hand. When she came to the copy of *They Were Expendable* I had rented from the video store, she stopped and stared a moment at the cover. John Wayne, Donna Reed, a PT boat and a palm tree.

"This is the most fucked movie," she said.

I was stung. I had rented it when she wasn't coming back, when I thought that useless bravery was a beautiful thing, grace under exterminating pressure. When I thought that was what I had left to me.

"I love that movie," I told her.

"Sure you do," she said. "The guys all get to be heroes."

"So does the girl," I said.

"But they escape," she said. "The boys all get off scot-free."

"No they don't."

"Sure they do. Do you even bother to watch these things?"

"You're wrong," I told her.

But Eleanor was right. The next night she had a dinner date with a friend from out of town, long-standing and un-rearrangeable, and while I waited for her (she promised to come by afterward) I watched the movie. And most of it was as I remembered: that same high false sentiment, that grit and bravery. I knew it was all fake but I believed it, too, and it seemed that that was what had gotten me through. But then, in the end, Eleanor was right: the men get onto a plane and go to teach the others how to fight the Japanese. In the end, they were not expendable. In the end, John Wayne escapes.

No Place in This World for You

MY SON'S NAME IS WALTER, he is four years old, and he bites other children. He does not bite them often. He does, though, bite them hard enough to draw blood, when he does bite.

His teeth are animal, tiny and sharp. When not upset, he is a placid boy, sleepy and sensitive, hungry for touch. He loves to be swaddled, loves to be held. My wife, Carol-Ann, nursed him for months and into years, until his first teeth came in, until top tooth met bottom tooth for the first time with her nipple in between and that was the end of that.

I am showing a house, a vintage adobe in Sam Hughes that was recently renovated at great expense and needs to sell soon, when my telephone goes off.

"It's Walter," says Carol-Ann.

My clients, my prospective buyers, are watching me apprehensively. A moment ago they were tranquil, almost home, admiring the granite countertops. Now something in my face has upset them.

"Can it wait?" I ask.

"Of course it can wait," she says. "I'll just go get him."

Why is she angry with *me*? It's my work, my persistence, that keeps us in Pampers and gasoline and trips to the Mexican Riviera.

"I'll be home soon, sweetie," I say, as brightly as I can muster, and the Drake twosome perks up. Carol-Ann disconnects without further words. The sun shines long and brightly across the freshly polished Saltillo-tile floors, and the smell of cookies lingers in the air. The sense of home is made of many small illusions and impressions, the solid thunk of an oak-and-iron door closing behind you, the light from the dining room sconces, the cool of thick walls on a hot morning.

I can never quite find a house that will keep Carol-Ann satisfied for long. It's always the wrong neighbors, or too much traffic. Our last house, it was a cat, basically a kitten, that ran out into the street after a lizard and got squashed by an Expedition. Little Muffin was the last straw for the house on Calle Negro. And the thing is, I'm in the business, I always make money when we sell, I always buy for a good price, a nice house in a nice area. This place we're in now, sits on half an acre, with a pool and a nice shady patio. But it's hard to feel settled.

I walk in through the front door and Walter rushes to meet me, *Daddy! Daddy!* and a hug around the leg. I think for a moment that he's trying to get himself off the hook but it isn't so. He's just glad to see me in an uncomplicated way. I put my hand on his little head and I love him. I wish everything was this uncomplicated. My heart goes out.

"The end of my rope," says Carol-Ann. "The end of my fucking rope."

She's sitting in the mottled shade of the ramada, a glass of sparkling water in her hand. Walter has gone back to his evening television trance. I pour a glass of wine for myself and sit across from her. I know better than to try and touch her.

"Who was it this time?"

"It was that nice little Wentworth girl," she says. "The little blonde one. I guess she took a toy car that he was playing with."

"There's nothing wrong with that. It's not her fault."

"No," says Carol-Ann, and looks at me like I'm crazy. "No, of course not. It's just learning to play with others, that's what they're supposed to be doing, isn't it? He got her right on the arm."

"How bad?"

"They had to go to the emergency room," says Carol-Ann. "I mean, they didn't *have* to, it wasn't anything major, but it did break the skin. I guess there was a little blood."

"Christ."

"The parents totally freaked out. They said they were going to sue the Tiny Tots."

"You can't sue over something like that. It's just kids being kids."

"I don't know," says Carol-Ann. "The mom's a lawyer. We'll see. They were gone to the hospital by the time I got there."

"Well, thank god for that."

"Oh, yeah," says Carol-Ann. "It was a lucky break."

"I wonder—" I start to say, but Carol-Ann stops me. I track her eyes and see that Walter has come out onto the patio behind me. Like a sleepwalker he ambles in my direction, studying the ground in front of his feet. He was almost a month premature but I don't think that's got anything to do with anything. A month is nothing these days. When he was in the neonatal ICU there was a baby in there the size of a squirrel. I mean exactly the size. Walter climbs sleepily into my lap and rests his head against my neck. In the still evening, the animal heat of his body against mine, his hot breath on my neck starts me sweating. It's almost too much, his dense, damp love.

"I didn't mean to," Walter says.

"I know."

"It was an accident."

"I know," I say again; although you can't bite somebody by accident, we both know that.

Carol-Ann suddenly leaps to her feet.

"I'm going to go for a run," she says. "I've been cooped up in the AC all day!"

"It's almost dark."

"It's almost cool enough," she says. "You two can rustle up dinner for yourselves, can't you?"

"We can wait."

"No, go ahead," she says. "There's all kinds of stuff in the freezer if you get desperate. Maybe you can go to Sanchez, get a burrito."

She goes in to change, leaves us sweating in the twilight. Out in the desert, things are stirring, all the predatory nightlife. Walter doesn't have anything to say to me, and I can't think of anything to say to him. Bad boy. Biter. That last cat, the one after Muffin, we found her off in the wash behind the house, stiff as a board. The vet said a rattlesnake must have got her. Walter was the one who found her. I think we're done with cats for a while.

"You two have fun!" says Carol-Ann, already sweating a little in her spandex, her little purple water bottle strapped to the small of her back. "Boys' night," she says, and starts to run, right there in the backyard, around the corner of the house and gone. I watch her ass as it goes. She has a lovely ass, a lovely girl, she really keeps herself in shape.

"Mom!" says Walter, who has just now discovered she was going, I think. He leaps off my lap. It's a painful cry, and I expect her to come comfort him before she goes, but Carol-Ann is already gone.

"It's OK, buddy," I tell him. "She'll be back pretty soon."

He looks momentarily lost, staring at the place where she left, as if she were just hiding around the corner of the house, but she's gone, gone, gone. We go inside, then, seal the house against the evening heat and turn the air on, cool and quiet as an operating room. Walter vegetates in front of PBS until the *Business Report* comes on, at which point I switch the show over to Atlanta, the Braves and the Marlins. I grew up in Alpharetta myself. It's something that we do, Walter and I, watch the Braves on TV. I crack a beer and get him a Juicy Juice. I don't know what Walter gets out of it but he seems to like it, leaning up next to me on the couch, he settles in and just lets the ball game go by. Smoltz is pitching tonight, it seems like he's been there forever. Chipper Jones, I remember when he was a rookie, just coming up. The Marlins take an early two-run lead. Walter and I wait for the Braves to come back. During the commercials, between innings, I get us chips and salsa, another beer for me. Walter asks if he can have a Coke but I tell him ask your mom, she ought to be home pretty soon. I wait dinner.

The seventh-inning stretch comes and I make us hot dogs. We eat them in front of the TV.

Those Southern girls. I see them at the ballpark with their boyfriends, big blonde hair, smooth legs in shorts and Atlanta Braves jerseys. They kiss their boyfriends, cheer for the strikeouts. Smoltz is really picking up his game in the late going. Those girls, they *defer.* Sometimes I think that's half the reason I watch these games, just to see the manners of the crowd, the little differences, so familiar to me. These girls don't walk into a restaurant first and pick out the table. They don't interrupt. It's just a different game, is all, and one I miss.

Nine o'clock, the game is over, the Braves have come from behind and Carol-Ann still isn't home. I bundle Walter off to the bath, have another beer while he messes around with his ducks and boats. His favorite part is when I come back, towel him off and then wrap him tightly in a big bath towel, tight as a mummy, and carry him down the hall to his bedroom. He seems smaller, more fragile, when he's bundled like this. I get him into his PJs and then we read a Curious George book and then I shut the light off.

Carol-Ann doesn't make it home till an hour later.

"What happened?" I ask her.

"Nothing *happened*," she says. "I went by Katherine's house on the way back and thought I'd stop by and say hello."

"Three hours ago."

"Yep," she says. "Three hours. I'm going to go take a shower."

I don't say anything. There doesn't seem to be anything to say. I wait till I hear the water running, open the last beer of the night and go down on the deck, down by the pool. The moon is out and sparkling on the water. I reach behind the chimenea and find the pack of cigarettes safely nestled in their plastic bag and I take one out and light it and watch the thousand stars wheel by overhead. Down in Tucson, splayed out in front of me like a river of light, police helicopters buzz and wheel, following their spotlights. Walter, Walter, I ask myself, what can we do with you? On the couch, watching the ball game, I had my arm wrapped around him, and without even thinking he took my free hand and brought it to his mouth and put his mouth on the knuckle of my index finger. He didn't bite down but I could feel his teeth. I left my finger there in his mouth. He is my son, after all.

Carol-Ann is already in bed when I get back up to the

house. I brush my teeth and shut the lights off and slip into bed beside her, the air in our bedroom as cool as the tomb. I slip my hand along the length of her side, covered in cotton jersey.

"Things will get better," I whisper.

"I don't know," she says without turning. Then, after a moment, she says, "Things will get different."

Then, a few minutes later, when I am sure she is asleep and I am awake beside her and thinking about money, she says, "I can feel it coming."

*　　*　　*

T H E Drakes are a gift from God, a faculty new hire with spousal accommodation, from Ohio. They have two fat salaries and a convert's enthusiasm for the place. They have been to the Desert Museum and walked the old streets of the barrio and gone to a couple of Sidewinders games under the lights, a hundred degrees at game time but cool as soon as the sun goes down.

They will certainly buy a house, and a nice one. They fell into my lap when Sally Drake sat in on a yoga class that Carol-Ann was taking and they started to talk about neighborhoods after: Sam Hughes is nice, keeps you out of the traffic, you can walk to work, but the shopping is so much better in the Catalina Foothills. . . . The next day they were in my office, friendly as golden retrievers. Six weeks later, they are still showing up. They have seen a perfectly nice house in every neighborhood in Tucson, a 250-year-old adobe downtown, a series of mini-mansions in Foothills, even a real one-off, a twenties movie-star palace in El Encanto, with a pool lined with hand-painted tile. They have liked them all, cheerfully and at length. They could afford any of them. They have bought none of them.

I know what their problem is, but I can't solve it for them. Each of them is waiting for the other to decide. They each want it to be the other one's fault if things turn out badly, which of course they will, at least in part. Nothing's perfect. There's something wrong with every house, with every life and every marriage. It's just a matter of balance. But Tom wants Sally to pick the house, to fall in love, to say finally that this is the one. When the pool starts to leak, he'll have somebody to blame, when their Ohio cats start falling prey to Arizona snakes, when that inaccessible lightbulb, twenty feet up in the cathedral ceiling, finally burns out.... And of course Sally wants Tom to make the pick. I started off thinking their sex life must have been awful, lying there in the dark and waiting for the other to make the first move. Lately I have changed my mind. Lately I've caught a whiff of passion from Sally; she's a little chunky, in a pleasant kind of way, nice and round, likes to eat, likes to listen to music. I imagine that they fight a lot, behind closed doors, and then they make up. Make-up sex is always the best.

Today we're looking at a house that they are not going to buy. I know this before we start and I think they know it, too. I'm trying to show them that I care, that I'm working hard for them. I don't know exactly what's in it for Tom and Sally. The house is actually nice, three wings built around a courtyard, and it shows really well; it's walled in from the street, just a blank line of stucco, then you get into the house and it's shady and cool and there, from every window of the house, is the courtyard with its fountain and greenery. The sound of trickling water everywhere, like some oasis. We shuffle slowly from room to room, taking it all in, winding up in the long, low living room, something shiplike in the lines, the oval mouth of an adobe fireplace in the corner.

"Well," I ask them. "What do you think?"

They look from one to the other and then to me, like this is some kind of a test.

"How long has it been on the market?" Sally asks.

"A few weeks," I tell her. "I'm a little surprised it's stuck around this long."

"It's not expensive," Tom says, pretending to think. "It is the nicest house on the block, though. The nicest house in a couple of blocks."

It's not about money, I want to tell them. It's about love. Buy any house and stay in it for a few years and you'll make your money. You need a place that will make you happy, a place to call home. But everybody wants to get a good deal, everybody wants to look smart, good with money. Tom and Sally Drake are no exception.

"I love that courtyard," Sally says. "But the neighborhood."

"It's not really walking distance to the university," Tom says.

"Rincon Market's just down the street," I tell them. "A nice little Sunday-morning stroll. And the schools are OK."

"Not that that matters to us," Tom says. At our first meeting weeks ago, he had announced that they were "child-free" and had every intention of staying that way.

"No," I say, "but in terms of resale value, it makes a difference. I think this area has a lot of upside potential."

I don't know why I talk like this: *upside potential.* It doesn't even mean anything. But it makes the clients feel better, smarter, in the loop. I watch Sally walk into the kitchen, touching the granite, the steel and glass. The light from the window behind her turns her summer blouse translucent, and I watch her body as she turns, slimmer than I had thought, still substantial. "I like the layout of this kitchen," she says. "It's very practical."

"Well, and it's a little smaller than some of the other places we've looked at," Tom says. "That's maybe a good thing—less to cool, less to heat. Assuming we'd fit."

"Oh, I think we'd fit fine," says Sally. "Put the offices over in that far wing, you wouldn't hear a thing."

"You like this place," Tom says.

"I'll have to sleep on it," says Sally.

"I'm worried about the neighborhood," says Tom.

* * *

T I M Hudson's on the mound tonight. Through the first three innings, he looks completely in charge, spotting his fastball on the microscopic edges of the plate and getting the calls. He's got the split-finger going for him, and a wicked curve. The

Mets start arguing called third strikes, looking like so many petulant children.

Walter snuggles next to me on the sofa, sucking pensively at the straw of his juice box. Carol-Ann's downstairs working against a deadline. She's a freelance graphic designer, does layout for a couple of special-market magazines, tonight I think it's *Gun Dog.* Either that or maybe *Contemporary Beverage.* Either way, she's behind the clock, she had Walter all day till I got home and I guess he wouldn't nap. I can hear her through the floor, she's got a nice studio with nice big windows and an exercise room right next door. She leaves the TV going while she works and sometimes she'll take a break for fifteen minutes on the elliptical trainer or a session with the free weights. She says it clears her mind. I can hear the rhythm through the floor.

Top of the fourth, the telephone rings. I get up to answer it but Walter clings to me, I have to disentangle my arm from his hot, sticky grip. I almost miss the call.

"Is this Walter's dad?" says the pleasant voice on the other end.

"Yes, it is."

"Ted Wentworth here," he says, and a physical dread runs through me. I don't want to do this. He says, "I know you heard about the incident yesterday."

"I did. I want you to know that I'm very, very sorry."

"No, no, that's all right," says Ted Wentworth. "I just wanted to establish a couple of things, you know. Points of information. First off, did you or did you not tell the Tiny Tots

Center that your son had a history of this kind of, ah, be-havior?"

I stand there with my mouth hanging open and nothing to say, Walter staring at me, puzzled. Of course we didn't tell them. They never would have let him near the place if they had known. The world hates a biter.

"I'd have to ask my wife," I finally say. "She did most of the, uh, when we were setting it up. . . ."

"You didn't discuss it with her?"

"I don't remember doing so."

"You don't remember? That seems like an important point. Maybe you can check with her."

"As soon as she gets back," I say.

"When will that be?"

"Not for a few days," I tell him. "Her mother isn't doing well. Carol-Ann had to go help out."

"I hope it's nothing serious," says Ted Wentworth. "Give her my best, when you talk to her. And ask her, would you? when you talk to her? It's kind of an important point. The Tiny Tots people say they never had a clue about it. According to them, you never said a thing. But maybe your wife will be able to shed some light on this."

"When she gets back," I say.

"When she gets back," he says. He doesn't believe me. "Or when you talk to her. I'll check back in a day or two."

"Did you want us—" I say. "I mean, I'd be glad to pay the hospital or whatever."

"That's not the direction we're going in right now," says Ted

Wentworth. "I'll let you know if anything changes and I look forward to hearing from you soon. Have a lovely evening."

I slip the phone back into the charger gently, as if it might explode or worse. Walter looks up at me. He's sensitive as a candle flame to changes in mood, he knows a feeling from across the room without having to talk about it. Right now he's worried about me. He sees the way I look at him, like a stranger. Where did he come from? What's wrong with him? But, really, nothing. He is my boy, loving and warm and worried.

He sees me flinch as the phone rings again. I wonder if I have the nerve to answer it.

But it isn't Wentworth, it's the familiar cell phone with the Ohio prefix, and I answer cheerfully.

"Hello, Sally!" I say. "What is up?"

"That house?" she says. "That one we looked at today? I think I'd like to take another look at it. It's kind of grown on me, that courtyard and that fountain and all. And I think Tom's more and more OK with it."

"Terrific!" I say, though I don't believe her for a minute. This is so completely the wrong house for them. It's a family place, designed with the master suite at one end and the children's rooms at the far extremity; a place designed for quiet, for sleeping in, even for marital sex while the children sleep. But I don't tell her. "I'll call the listing agent in the morning," I tell her. "What time's good for you?"

"Eleven?"

"Eleven it is," I tell her. "See you then."

*   *   *

B U T when I call the listing agent in the morning, she tells me there's a binding offer on the property, sold pending financing, and the financing looks good. *You never know*, I tell Sally, but her faith in me is shaken. She's polite but curt when I call to tell her. I understand, too late, that this is what it took to get them to make a decision: the only way to stir their desire was if someone else desired it more. They could want it after all, but somebody else had to want it first.

I don't hear from them for a few days afterward and nothing pressing comes across the MLS. I've got other fish to fry, anyway. The house in Sam Hughes isn't moving, and all my cash is tied up in that one. I've got my eye on a rental in the student ghetto north of the U, a nice old house that's been subdivided into a rabbit hutch of individual rooms. It's an eyesore but the cash flow is awesome. If I can get out from under the place in Sam Hughes, I could be turning $1500 a month just off this one property.

So I'm motivated. I drop the price by $10,000 and schedule an open house on Sunday. At the last minute, Carol-Ann decides that she's too far behind in her work, after watching Walter at home all week. She decides that I need to bring Walter along with me to the open house. This is what? We don't fight in front of Walter, but she knows I need room to move. It's a delicate business. The last thing a prospective buyer wants to see is a four-year-old in an empty room. With him along, it's going to be a total waste of time, this afternoon, and

Carol-Ann knows it, or ought to know it. But she says, *He's your child, too.* She says, *I'm not the only one.* We haven't even talked about where we might place him next. So I bundle up a blanket and a little chair and several books and snacks and most importantly the portable DVD player and a few choice Disney disks and set him up in the back bedroom—a child's bedroom, anyway, so he won't look out of place. Walter looks worried in this strange house. He doesn't want me to leave the room. But I have business.

It's slow, a trickle of tire kickers. It's the first day under a hundred for the last weeks and maybe months, the first inkling that fall may someday come. Clouds are gathering in the distance for an afternoon thunderstorm and everybody is restless, prickly, slightly electric. You can feel it coming, some kind of change. I go back to check on Walter and find him standing at the window, staring out at the gravel yard, the giant tortured prickly pear rising out of the center of it.

Four o'clock and I'm about to wrap things up when Sally Drake comes through the door. She doesn't see me at first, doesn't know this is my open house. And she's not supposed to be looking at houses without me. It's not a deal killer but it is against the rules. I'm with another prospect, talking about utility bills, so I let her wander by herself. She's been all through the house when she comes back to the kitchen, where I am alone, and she is surprised to find me.

"Sally," I say.

She looks caught but not contrite. She says, "I didn't real-

ize this was your property. I'm surprised you haven't shown it
to us."

"It didn't seem right for you."

"Well, you were right about that!" she says brightly. "Is
that your son back there?"

"Walter."

"You might want to go have a look at him," Sally says. "He
might be crying. He looked pretty upset, anyway."

She's watching me, to see if I leap up, abandon my business, run to his side. I don't know what she wants me to do.
Walter looks like that a lot, especially to strangers. To me it's
just his usual face, his usual expression. But others see it differently.

"He's a good-looking boy," says Sally Drake. Something
about her is softening. It's always Tom, and never Sally, who
uses that phrase *child-free*. She's a good-looking woman in her
middle thirties, it's not too late for her.

"I'd better check on him," I say. "I'm sure he's all right."

"I'm going to go now," says Sally, strangely definite.

"Where's Tom?"

"Oh, he's at orientation, all this week. He said that he could
take a break, though, anytime, if something came up. He said
to tell you that, if I talked to you."

"OK," I tell her. "Good."

But watching her go, I feel like something's leaving with
her, I can't say what but just a lessening. The house is empty
now, empty but for me and Walter. I go out onto the lawn and I

pull the Open House sign down and bring it inside and lock the door. I go back to check on him then and he is staring, again, out that back window. Walter is Walter, by which I mean that he is fine, he is doing fine. But there is some elemental sadness in him. It is his deep constitution, I think, and unreachable. Maybe that's it, I think, as I reach down to pick him up. Maybe it's just an endless need for comfort, a need that can't be satisfied except in the moment that it is. In my arms he is pliant and comfortable, a deep slow breather. In my arms and in his mother's arms and maybe nowhere else.

He is a puzzle, my son.

At home, Carol-Ann is waiting. She says, "I talked to Ted Wentworth this afternoon."

Walter is sleeping. He went out in the car seat on the way home. I walk softly with his limp weight in my arms, across the living room and down the corridor to his room, where I lay him gently as I can into his race-car bed. When I come out again into the living room, I see Carol-Ann outside on the patio, waiting for me. Get me out of here, I think. Take me home.

"It's just so *stupid*," Carol-Ann says. "You made me sound like an *idiot*. My *mother*."

"No," I tell her. "It wasn't the best idea."

"What were you thinking?"

"Ah," I say. I wait and gather myself; and in that momentary wait I realize that I am angry myself, she's not the only one, I'm not going to bow down. "I was thinking," I tell her, "that we had never told the center about Walter's problem. I was thinking we were totally screwed. We're going to get sued, babe."

"So you make up some idiotic story."

"It wasn't my best moment. He caught me by surprise, is all."

"I don't want to do this," she says.

"What?"

"Any of it," Carol-Ann says. "I'm going for a run."

"You're going to get rained on."

"I don't care," she says, and goes inside to change. A minute later, I hear the front door shut, a solid, heavy sound that I've always liked. She's gone. The clouds are gathering themselves into something heavy, something big. I decide to let Walter sleep for now. I go up to our bedroom, where her clothes are flung across our unmade bed, and I change into my swimsuit, and look at myself in the mirror. I am not bad for thirty-seven, I think, a little fatter around the middle than I was at seventeen but still presentable. I go back out into the heat of late afternoon and the swirl of sunlight and clouds and in one motion I cross the patio and dive headfirst into the pool, where I lie underwater for as long as I can, savoring the sudden, enveloping cool. I surface for breath and then dive again, and again.

*   *   *

SOMETIMES it seems to me that anger is the engine of a marriage, the power that drives all the other parts. Each of us is doing half and feeling like it's three-quarters. Each of us has it exactly as hard as the other, and suspects the other of having it easy. Both of us take care, and suspect the other of carelessness. I can hear her down in the basement, the rhythmic squeak of the elliptical trainer . . . I need to get down there and grease that thing, one of these days.

The listing agent calls after dinner Monday night, says the financing's looking a little shaky on the courtyard house and now might be a good time to get in a backup offer. Is this good news? It might be, now that the Drakes have declared their love for the place, or at least their interest. But something has happened between myself and the Drakes, some small erosion of trust, and they're going to wonder if I am trying to trick them into a decision.

It's Tom who answers the phone. "Good news," I tell him, and let him know it's available. I explain what a backup offer is and how it works and why it might not be such a bad idea, if they're interested, to get something on paper before the current buyer gets his financing straight.

"I'm still a little worried about the neighborhood," he says. He sounds less than thrilled by the news. He says, "Look, let me talk to Sally and I'll get right back with you, OK?"

"No hurry," I tell him—and I mean it, no hurry, this guy's never going to buy this house from me or any other house, he's just going to pull my chain until I'm dead, or till they move back to fucking Ohio. I'm tempted to tell him. Instead I suggest that he have a nice evening.

Walter and I are watching the Dodgers tonight. The Braves

are not on the national network and this is the only game on. Carol-Ann is "working." In a minute. Sally Drake calls back to say that Tom is all tied up in his orientation meeting but she could meet me at the house in the morning. This means no, of course. If they were going to buy it, they would both make a point of being there. But I set it up for eleven the next day anyway, because to do otherwise would be to acknowledge a difficult truth. As long as we don't say anything, it will all be fine.

In the morning, Carol-Ann says she can't take care of Walter.

It's all right, I tell her, and in a way it is. I'm not selling a house anyway, not this morning. I bundle up all of Walter's things, his toys and books, a change of clothes, a snack, some drink boxes, the DVD and a few disks, I move the car seat from Carol-Ann's car to mine and think that Hannibal brought less crap with him when he invaded Europe and I'm thinking that somewhere in here she's got to talk. Not once have we talked. Neither of us has any idea what happens next, to Walter, to our busy working lives. It seems to me that we are not in this together.

"What were you doing last night?" I ask her, when we are finally packed. "I thought you were working."

"I was," she says. "It's not like I just fall off a log and there's a magazine. It's a lot of work. You know that."

"OK, OK, OK."

"It's just, you sniping at me."

"OK," I say, and get out of there. It seems like there's no part of our life that's not anger, not now.

I'm making excuses.

I get there early, get Walter all set up in the living room with his blanket and Juicy Juice and Ninja Turtles. He loves the fucking Ninja Turtles. I should explain that the sellers of the house have rented a houseful of dummy furniture, to make the place look lived in, which in this case was a mistake. The house is all dark wood and cream plaster and iron brackets and the furniture is totally Miami Beach. But they're not buying it anyway and I don't care if Walter slobbers Kiwi Strawberry all over the upholstery. It couldn't be worse than it already is. I leave him there with his little brain sucked into the DVD player and I go outside to turn on the fountain. The courtyard fills with the sound of water.

Sally shows up five minutes early, looking what? looking *caught* again, as she was at the open house, abstracted, blankly smiling. She shakes my hand and then she tousles Walter's hair, waking him from the video dream for just a surprised moment before he slides back under. I should be ashamed and I am, to let him go this way. But I have work to do.

We leave Walter in the living room and make the rounds of the house again, the children's bedrooms—which I am careful to refer to as offices—and back past the one fairly bad bathroom (a leaky shower stall has led to pulled linoleum) and through the main areas of the house. We shuffle slow as sleepwalkers and Walter either doesn't notice us as we pass or just chooses to ignore us. The kitchen is lovely, the covered patio in back. Sally oscillates between evasive and merely noncommittal. Her enthusiasm is gone, though, and we both know it. At the end of things, we wind up in the master bedroom, all dark wood and half-light through the heavy, partly drawn curtains. We have run out of house, run out of things to say or ways to distract ourselves.

"It's all wrong, isn't it?" I ask her.

"I don't know," she says. "It just felt different the other day."

When you couldn't have it, I think. But I don't say it.

"There's something wrong with us," she says. She draws the heavy bloodred curtain back and stares out into the courtyard, the blinding late-morning sunlight turning all the colors pale, washing every color out in its white heat. Even the trickling water sounds hot.

"It's a stressful time," I say. "Transitions are hard."

"Three moves equals a death," she says. "I read that somewhere."

"I've heard that before."

"It's not that," she says. She turns from the window, lets the curtain slip half closed again, the light retreating quickly from the room.

"I hate it here," she says. There it is again, the anger, the thing between men and women. She's trembling with anger. She says, "I never wanted to leave Ohio. The part we lived in was nice, you know, down near Kentucky. Everybody thinks about Ohio and they think, you know, Akron. Cleveland. But where we lived, it wasn't like that at all."

"Summer will be over pretty quick," I tell her. "A few more

weeks and we'll be out of the heat. We're out of the worst of it already."

"It's like living on the moon," she says. "I burned my hand on my own steering wheel the first week we were here. *Burned* it."

"I'm sorry."

"It's just weather," she says. "I don't care about weather."

It's like I suddenly see her, like I can look into her eyes now, and see into her, instead of stopping at the opaque surface. A moment ago she was part of the furniture, a thing among things. Now she stands awkwardly in front of me, not knowing what to say or where to put her body, and I can see into her, the bleeding core.

I don't know why, I take her hand.

"It'll be OK," I tell her.

"Tom had an affair," she says.

"I'm sorry," I tell her.

"That's not the problem," Sally says.

I'm suddenly aware of the king-size bed looming next to us, like a big lewd joke.

She says, "The problem is, we decided to make a new start, stick together. We knew we couldn't do it if we stayed. We tried, and things were unraveling pretty fast. I love him, you know that?"

"I always thought you did."

"But just to have to be so *positive* all the time," she says. "So fucking constructive! Sometimes I think, you know, I'm not going to forgive him, not really, I mean I don't go a day without remembering. I'm not going to forget, either. So what am I doing here?"

I don't have an answer.

The quiet all around us, the plash of water.

Sally looks down at our hands, joined together, then looks up into my eyes and I see there is a world in there, behind her eyes, a world as big and complicated as my own. And I see that she means to be kissed, for whatever reasons she has, and I feel my dick stir at the thought of her, the nearness. I pull her close with my free hand and kiss her very softly, as gently as I can, because this woman needs gentle treatment. She deserves it. Her mouth tastes of cigarette smoke and mints.

And this embrace, this entanglement is where we are when Walter comes into the room. She sees him first and drops from my arms in one of those graceful, rapid, womanly moves, like a woman taking off a swimsuit. She stands staring and I turn and I see him, then.

"Hey, buddy," I say.

Small and worried and upset, he stands in the bedroom doorway, looking from my face to Sally's and back again.

"Come here," I say, and bend down to receive him, and he doesn't move. Then slowly, always slowly, little worried Walter drops his blanket and walks toward me, the slow underwater motion and his frightened eyes and as he passes Sally she reaches to do what? to touch his hair, perhaps, to comfort him, and before I can stop her, in dreamlike slow motion, he turns his pretty head toward her hand and bites her, bites the soft wide flesh below her thumb, bites her hard and sharp enough to draw blood and as Sally starts to shriek I think, Walter my love, Walter my life, Walter my only son, what will we ever do with you? Because the world hates a biter, and my love cannot protect you.

Sleeping Beauty

ANDREW STANDS AT THE WINDOW looking out at the dark street, waiting for his friends: Susan and Ray, Elizabeth and Mark. They're late. The married are always late. He has made everything ready for them: candles lit, wine decanted, a spinach salad ready for dressing and the makings of a seafood risotto circled around the new gas stove. This is his one trick, risotto, but they say they like it. They finish it, anyway. And on a night like this one, dark and threatening snow, it's a good thing, warm and filling, a little breeze out of the south. . . .

Then they arrive, all together in Elizabeth's minivan. He lets the curtain slip back so he won't be caught looking, starts the Rubén González CD he was saving for them and waits. A suspended moment, his own little quiet, waiting for the Cuban piano. He can hear the married talking in the building's hallway.

Then kisses, coats, and now they're all together. A sense of relief.

"The new place," Susan says. "Andrew, this is great."

"Ah," he says, half embarrassed. "It's almost done, almost finished, always almost."

"No, it's beautiful," says Elizabeth. "Let me see." She rushes past him into the one big room, taking it all in: the fire in the fireplace, the bookshelves and the sofa, the big lithograph of the Yellowstone River at dawn on the one good wall. He can't, suddenly, stand to watch her taking the room apart, the work of months. He gathers the coats and retreats to the bedroom and then she's there, too, after just a minute, gathering in all the details: the big bed in dark wood, the telephone, the high-fidelity clock.

"You did it," Elizabeth says. "You really made something beautiful out of this place. It looks wonderful."

She says it with absolute certainty. Andrew wonders what she would have said if she didn't like it, then instantly wonders if she really does like it. But she circles him in her arm and kisses him on the cheek and she does, she does like it.

"It looks like somebody lives here," she says. "No more college-student. It was time."

"Past time," he says. "You like the color in here?"

"I ought to," she says. "I picked it out, didn't I?"

And then Susan is in the room, too, appreciating.

"Wow," she says. "This is really nice, Andrew. You did this all by yourself?"

"I had some help," Andrew says.

Susan says, "You're going to have seductions in here, is my prediction."

"I didn't do anything," Elizabeth says. "I helped with the colors a little."

"I don't know," says Andrew. "Do women like men with furniture?"

Both women stop, consider.

"Grown-up women do," Elizabeth says. She's talking about Jude, Andrew's what?—*ex-girlfriend* seems too vague and too definite all at once. Jude who is now in Cyprus with somebody else but always a threat to return. A little spanking, thank you very much. Elizabeth never liked Jude in the first place but now that Jude has been back and gone and back and gone again, Elizabeth thinks it's Andrew's problem. Jude's not going to change, it's true, he thinks, looking at the faces of the women he's known for years. But neither of you has ever taken me to the nude beach.

"What if I don't like grown-up women?" Andrew says.

"You like us, don't you?" Elizabeth says. "We're not just grown-up, we're old, we're all wrinkly and everything."

And something happens here, something happens to Susan, a little cloud, and Elizabeth looks embarrassed. She's said the wrong thing, Andrew thinks. What?

In the living room, Ray is wrestling open a bottle of red

wine, a bottle he brought, sure, but still Andrew feels that his rights as host have been violated. My house, my wine-bottle opener. They are taking over from him, here in his own little place—a place he built in part to prove that he was one of them, a grown-up as Elizabeth put it, even if he wasn't coupled. They've known one another since college, Ray and Andrew and Elizabeth. Mark came later, and Susan, and Jude, and then they had all disappeared into the mysterious closed houses of their marriages, leaving him outside.

"Did Susan tell you?" Mark asks Andrew.

"What?"

"The accident," he says, and everybody turns to look at Susan, and Susan blushes, which is not like her at all. She's an ER nurse, tough, coarse, funny.

"Some girl out of nowhere," she says. "I was just driving through Tenley Circle on Wisconsin Avenue and this girl, I don't know if she was stoned or what, she says she never even saw the light and I believe her. She came through the red light at thirty miles an hour and hit me right on the door."

"Jesus," Andrew says. "Are you . . ."

"No, it's not that," Susan says. "I mean, thank god for Volvo, you know? Old as that thing was."

"What did she say?" Mark asks her. "The girl that hit you. Did you get a chance to talk to her?"

"Oh, it was bad," Susan says. "She must have broken her nose, I think, I mean there was blood running all down her face and I was OK, you know? Or at least I thought I was

OK, the weird part is you can't really tell if you remember everything or not. But this girl is bleeding all over herself and following me around going I'm sorry, I'm sorry."

"Sorry about what?" Ray says. "Sorry I almost killed you? I mean, seriously, fuck you."

"That's right," says Susan. "Fuck you."

A silence, in which Ray lines up five wineglasses and solemnly pours the bottle empty, dividing the wine between them. Ceremony, Andrew thinks. He can feel the party slipping away from him, turning into something else. Maybe it was supposed to.

"So," Elizabeth says, and they all touch glasses. "To life."

"No," says Mark. "Not to life in general. I want to drink to Susan, to this particular life which is still being lived, thank god. I mean, all of us, but today it's this one, particular . . . I don't know what I'm talking about."

"No, you're right," says Andrew, and they all sip their wine, Andrew looking at Mark in the warm light, thinking that when Mark said thank god he meant a real God, a present one. That's why Elizabeth loved him, he thought—not cynical like the rest of them, a thinker, a believer, a volunteer at the homeless shelter. A doer of good.

"It's like you're on the tightrope all the time and you don't even know it," Ray says. "Then something happens and you realize."

Susan looks at him, a flash of anger. This is her story.

"Then you forget again," says Elizabeth.

"I don't think so," Susan says. "Not anytime soon."

"We were admiring your place," Mark says to Andrew, a neat conversational side step. "It's a lot of work."

"You should have seen the place when he bought it," Elizabeth says.

"It wasn't that bad," Andrew says.

"No," says Mark. "I just admire the way that you've made a place for yourself, just really seen it through and made it so nice. I don't know if I would."

"You might," says Susan. "Ray wouldn't."

"Hey," Ray says.

"Well, would you?"

"Probably not," he says. "I'd just move into my studio, set up a hot plate."

"Or find some girl to take care of you," Susan says.

"Or find some girl," he says. But it's not quite a joke, they are not laughing together, they aren't even looking at each other. Andrew smiles as if it was a joke and takes his wine into the kitchen.

My kitchen, he thinks.

I don't know if I would, Mark said. You wouldn't have to, Andrew thinks. He puts the big enameled pot on the burner, lights the flame underneath. You have a home, you have Elizabeth, you have *daughters*. The others are laughing in the next room and Andrew is cutting the butter into pats, watching it start to melt. The others are talking, a low indistinguishable murmur. You have each other, you take care of each other. Andrew isn't even sure he wants these nice things, although he has been able to afford them for some time. And it was, OK, it was ridiculous for him to be living in that one room and eating off the card table, sleeping on a mattress on the floor. And it makes money sense to own a place instead of renting.

But still.

It feels like surrender: all the life he is going to have. He pours in a little of the extra-good olive oil, waits for it to heat, then stirs in the carefully minced shallots. The smell fills the tiny kitchen, shallots in butter.

"Do you have any gin?" Susan asks.

She's there in the doorway, blonde and fair—not fragile, though, a big healthy Dutch girl—but her eyes are pink-rimmed like bunny eyes and Andrew sees that she's been crying. He missed it in the dim living room.

"Plenty," he says. "Three kinds. How do you want it?"

"In a glass," she says.

"You want ice?"

"I don't care," she says. "I want gin."

"I know that feeling," Andrew says, and turns the pot down to low, so that it won't burn, and takes one of the nice blue-rimmed Mexican glasses—the ones Elizabeth helped him pick out—and fills it with ice at the refrigerator. This movement, down to the far end of the little room, draws Susan deeper into the kitchen so that when he goes back for the gin—this is a one-butt kitchen—he has to brush against her. Susan turns toward him, not away. As he tries to pass she blocks him with her body. A stop, then Susan puts her arms around his waist and draws him to her body. Andrew doesn't know what this is. He folds his arms around her shoulders and lets her rest there, her head on his shoulder. She isn't saying anything. She isn't crying. Andrew can feel the outlines of her body through the layers of clothes, she's up against him with the whole length of her body, pressing, breasts and hips. This is something, Andrew thinks. This is not hello or good-bye or good to see you but something else. And then it goes on. It goes on longer, Susan holding him, holding him with the length of her body until Andrew can imagine her, heavy and full and pale-pink, fair. He thinks of Jude, dark skin, dark hair, the last time. And then the shallots—he can smell them—start to caramelize, which is not right. But he can't let go. Although she isn't weeping, he still can't turn her from his arms; and then, too, he isn't sure he wants to. It's been a while since he's been held by anyone, and there's a comfort in it, a place for rest, protection, he could stay here, even if it's really nothing, he could stay . . . except the shallots are coloring, he can smell them, in a minute they will start to burn and the butter will burn and he doesn't have any more shallots, even if he wanted to start over.

"Sorry," he whispers, loosening his hold on her. He expects her to let go but she doesn't.

"Sorry," he says again, and pulls his body slowly from hers, leaving them both empty-handed in the little vacant kitchen. She isn't looking at him. She isn't looking anywhere.

Andrew stirs the shallots, a little late but they're all right, they'll have to do, stirs the careful bowl of rice into the butter and oil and stirs to coat.

When he turns back she's still standing there, abandoned. He takes her hand and she seems to come to life—looks at him, smiles regretfully, squeezes his hand and lets go.

"I'm sorry," she says.

"I had to tend to the dinner," Andrew says. "I was afraid it would burn."

"No," Susan says. "No, that's fine. I'm better now."

Andrew stirs the pot while she pours herself a glass of gin, waits for her to come clean, to tell him. What just happened? He's glad to be of use but he'd like to know why.

"We looked at a place in Rockville the other day," Susan says.

"Rockville," Andrew says. "Rockville? What's wrong with your place?"

"Nothing," she says. "Ray'd like to have a studio in the house instead of working at the university all the time. But there's nothing wrong with our place."

Susan isn't going to tell him anything.

"Besides," she says, "we can't afford it."

"It's more than you think, isn't it?" he says, polite meaningless noise. "Everything is so expensive now."

"It really is," says Susan, drifting out of the doorway like smoke, back into the other room, back in with the others, the marriages.

Andrew regards his pot of rice.

Women and their mysteries.

They come, they go, they sleep with you or they don't, they go away, they put their head on your shoulder and press their bodies into yours and then they leave without explanation. Or maybe they tell everybody else. Maybe they just don't tell Andrew.

If only he were mysterious himself. But Andrew is plain as a potato, naked in his needs. The world knows what he wants.

"That smells terrific," Mark says. "How are you on the wine front?"

"I'm fine, I'm fine."

"Anything you need me to do?"

"Not really," Andrew says.

"What do you hear from Jude?" Mark asks.

Exhibit A: plain as a potato.

"I got an e-mail the other day," Andrew says. "She's working as a tutor for the son of the brother of the ex-president of Turkey, if I got that straight."

"How does she like it?"

"She does and she doesn't. The boy is fine but she doesn't like the servants' quarters, she says she'd rather be out in the dining hall with the movie stars."

"That sounds like Jude," Mark says. "She will be, too."

"What?"

"Out with the movie stars."

"Maybe," Andrew says. He does not wish to be sympathized with. "How about you?" he says.

"Nothing special," Mark says. "Nothing much. What are you doing for the holidays?"

"I don't know. I want to go to Thailand or someplace, someplace they've never heard of Jesus or Santa Claus."

"And what are you really going to do?"

"The usual, probably—go visit Mom in the nursing home and then come over to your house and drink too much. See who she thinks I am this time. Last month I was her brother Ernie, the one who died in Korea."

"Well, you're invited, definitely," Mark says.

"I did just invite myself, didn't I?"

"No," says Mark. "It's just that I think, it's not all squared away yet, but I think we might be going skiing with Elizabeth's family over the break. It's really the only chance, you know, with Emily in school now and all. I never realized how much of a schedule that put you on."

Andrew is stung, abandoned again. It's ridiculous, yes. And it's not their job to make a life for him but still.

"You know what Christmas is?" Andrew says, and Mark shrugs. "Christmas is just a big conspiracy to make single people feel shitty. That's why I want to go to Thailand, I mean, they probably have the exact same thing over there but at least I wouldn't understand it. It's like that thing, you see it in the paper all the time about how people need to get touched by other people at least three times a day or something starts to go wrong with them."

"You don't think that's true?"

"It's fucking married-person propaganda, Mark."

"Gee whiz," says Mark. "You want a hug or something?"

"Fuck off," says Andrew, happy again.

"Maybe we need the help," Mark says. "It's harder than it looks, staying married."

"Where are you going skiing?"

"I don't want to tell you."

"Where are you going skiing, Mark?"

"Gstaad," Mark admits.

"Switzerland," Andrew says. "Get the fuck out of here."

"Well, it's not settled yet. But Elizabeth's brother, I guess his wife has got a place over there and the exchange rates are pretty good this year. It wasn't our idea."

"Switzerland," Andrew says.

"It's just going to be family, family, family," Mark says. "It's not going to be any real fun."

"Of course it's not," Andrew says, sliding the seafood into the steaming pot, the shrimps and sea scallops. "Maybe I should go, maybe I should take Elizabeth and the kids. Because I could really have fun in Gstaad, I think."

"You're welcome to it."

"Maybe we'll ask Elizabeth," Andrew says. "Get a couple of glasses of wine into her and see what she says. I would do it, Mark, I would do it in a heartbeat just to prove that it's possible, that a person could have a good time in Switzerland. Gather the troops, will you? This is done."

And then he's alone again and maybe it's the wine or maybe the food—the complicated steam rising out of the pot, the pink shrimp—or maybe something else entirely but Andrew is suddenly all right. He's there in his kitchen making dinner for his friends. He has made right choices and wrong ones but they have worked out and if his life is not at all as he had imagined it, if his life is short of what he had hoped for, it is at least all right and better than most. He has friends, he has money, he can treat people well and sometimes he has Jude, too. He gets the nice new plates out of the nice new cupboard and arranges the asparagus, the risotto, the parsley on each.

Parsley, he thinks. What am I doing here?

He can hear Jude's laughter.

Also it seems to him that this sudden influx of well-being may just be from Susan's touch, her body all along the length of his. Maybe they were right, whoever they were—maybe he was withering from a lack of touch, shriveling. Three times a day. Who will touch him three times a day?

"Oh," says Elizabeth, "oh, Andrew, this looks wonderful," and she leads the others, the marrieds, in a round of applause while Andrew blushes.

"It's just like Aeroflot," he says. "Everybody claps when you land just because you didn't crash."

"Oh, horseshit," Ray says. "We came to eat."

"Then eat," says Andrew, and they do.

Then it's back, this sense that it's all right. It's not just Andrew but the whole table is feeling it: they have come through, they are alive and well. Susan's accident reminds them how lucky they are. Outside the window is a winter's night, a cold world that goes on and on, and here they are inside, a fire, a little Cubanismo in the background, food and talk and maybe it's not all just stuff, the things he's bought, the plates and silver and glass, the mission-oak dining table. Maybe it's just machinery to produce exactly this: this quiet, this security.

The men are eating, anyway.

Elizabeth is taking small, occasional bites, not really putting a dent in her food. Susan is eating half of everything: half a shrimp, half a scallop, half a spear of asparagus. She messes up the rest, pushing it around on her plate, and I have made this for you, Andrew thinks. I meant this to sustain you.

Maybe Susan is pregnant, he thinks. Maybe they both are. He recognizes the distaste from Elizabeth, her pregnancies before, the way she would eat without appetite to keep from disappointing him.

Or maybe it's just not too good, though it tastes all right to him.

"I'm sorry," Susan says. "I can't . . ."

She pushes her plate away from her, begins to stand and then her feet come out from under her, like somebody cut the string, and she folds sideways against the table and onto the floor. Her dress catches on something as she falls and so she lies half undone on the floor, her legs naked to the waist and her plain blue cotton underwear showing.

"Jesus Christ," says Ray. But he sounds more angry than concerned, embarrassed, something. Is this what married life does to you? She's fallen and he's angry.

It's Elizabeth who reaches her first, Elizabeth who smooths the dress down over her naked legs.

"Are you all right?" she says.

And Susan says, "Please."

"Please what?"

"Please get away," she says, turning her head away from Elizabeth, looking through the tangled chair and table legs in the direction of the fire. Where there are no faces, Andrew thinks.

His turn to kneel beside her, and Ray on the other side.

"Did you hit your head?" Ray asks. "Are you OK?"

But Susan's eyes are closed, she won't talk, she can't, she starts to shake her head from side to side—gently, no and no and no—and from somewhere in her throat comes a humming or moaning sound through her closed lips, Andrew can feel it rather than hear it and the sound pierces him. Oh, you, he thinks. In pain. All at once, he sees her: impassioned, in pain, laid out on his nice clean floor. He finds her hand and she takes it, grips him tight and draws his hand to her throat and holds it there with both hands while she weeps.

Ray kneels ignored and angry on her other side.

She holds his hand like it was the last thing in the world.

Her pale, beautiful legs stretched out like a dead woman's. Her well of skepticism gone and in its place this mute, defenseless . . .

"I'll take her home," says Mark. "Unless you think she needs to go to the emergency room."

"She's all right," Ray says. "I think she's just exhausted."

As if she were not in the room; except for Andrew, who can feel the shiver of muscle and nerve as she tries to stop crying, tries to pull herself back into the room. Again and again, like heat lightning.

"I think she's fine," Ray says to Mark. "She checked out fine this afternoon."

Whatever else she might be, Andrew thinks, *fine* is not the word. Oh, you, he thinks, looking down into her closed face: Susan, whom he has taken for granted for so long, whom he has known and counted on—because it pleased her to be counted on—and now here she is changed.

Then she lets go of his hand and turns away from him, too. From all of them.

"She's all right," Ray says.

He stands up and, in a minute, Andrew does, too.

Susan's still lying on the floor. Elizabeth and Mark are having one of those wordless, impenetrable conversations that the married specialize in. The food half eaten on their plates.

"I think we'd better go," Ray says.

"I'll drive you," Mark says—and just for that moment Susan looks up at the two of them, the men, and she shines a little ray of anger and disgust at them. She wants nothing to do with them. Then closes down again.

"Come on," Elizabeth says, motherly. "Come on, Susan. It's been a terrible day, I know. We'll get you home, you'll be fine. Susan. Please."

Something about the cadence of the words, the motherly confidence: do this, do that, I know, follow me.

"I don't want to spoil the party," Susan says, sitting up.

"I'm worried about you," Elizabeth says.

"Let me just lie down," Susan says. "I'll be all right."

This is all in code. She's saying something and the others are hearing her but not Andrew. Her face, for instance, is not all right—her face is a wreck, blotchy and smeared.

"I think we should go," Ray says.

"I don't want to go," Susan says. "I just want to lie down. I'll be all right if I can just lie down for a minute."

"Of course you can," Andrew says. "Here."

Susan takes his hand and lifts herself from the floor, stands upright on her own two feet—to prove to Ray and Mark and Elizabeth that she can—and looks from face to face to face with an expression that Andrew, again, can't read.

Maybe it's just that she won't be told what to do. Maybe it's simple as that.

Andrew follows her into the bedroom, closes the door. Susan sits on the edge of the bed and folds her hands together into a tight knot in her lap and looks at her hands. Big capable hands, Andrew thinks. He's never seen her like this.

"I didn't mean to . . . ," Susan says.

"I know you didn't," Andrew says, without waiting for her to finish.

"I thought I'd be OK," she says, and her voice is small and wondering and unlike her. "I thought I'd just get through it."

"No," he says. "It's easy to underestimate, an accident like that."

"It's not the accident."

"No," he says. And thinks, What then? but doesn't ask.

Instead he kneels on the new carpet beside the bed and

takes her shoes off. She's wearing little black lace-up boots with heels, little black boots that seem to have more than one thing on their minds.

"I'm sorry I spoiled your party," she says.

"I don't know you very well, do I?" Andrew says.

She lets go, then, of Andrew's hand, brings her own back to clasp her own hand and it's time to go.

"You don't know anything," she says.

"Do you want the light on?"

"I'll get it in a minute," she says. "I'll be fine."

"All right, then," Andrew says, and gets up and slips out of the room. This is what it's like to have a child, he thinks—remembering his own mother, saying good night, leaving the room, the awful loneliness when she left and understanding, now for the first time, how a part of her was left behind with him....

The other three are sitting around the table still, looking like they had never seen one another before.

"How is she?" asks Elizabeth.

"She seems to be fine," Andrew says, taking his place again in front of his half-finished dinner. "Tired."

"Of course she is."

The others have all stopped eating, without finishing, but Andrew is suddenly hungry again. He pours his glass three-quarters full of the Italian red that Cipolato recommended to him and it really is good, heavy and perfumed and full. The risotto is good, too. Really, he doesn't care if the others like it or not, whether they're in a mood to eat or not. Andrew cooks for himself, Andrew eats.

"Did you look at her pupils?" Ray asks.

"Not specifically. I mean, I assume they were still there and all. I would have noticed if they were missing."

Ray looks angry, Elizabeth amused, Mark looks sorrowful that he would joke at a time like this.

"If there's a concussion," Mark says. "It's one of the things you look for, if the pupils are too big or different sizes. We don't know if she hit her head or not. She says she doesn't remember."

"She seems to be fine," Andrew says. "Upset."

And here they look from each other to each other, trading messages that Andrew can't understand.

"Who wouldn't be?" Elizabeth says.

"Coffee?" Andrew says.

And yes, they would all—it turns out—rather be somewhere else this evening, in some other company, they are not in the mood for one another, not after today. Andrew would like to be elsewhere himself, some restless impulse, the dispiriting sight of his own snug little home, which seems to be screaming to the world BACHELOR BACHELOR BACHELOR. What's next is the Hugh Hefner brocade robe with the satin collar. And the others, Andrew can only guess at. Elizabeth with her children, Ray off painting in his studio, Mark helping the homeless. Humping the helpless. Andrew's in a strange mood, now.

But they get through.

This has been going on for years now, ever since college. Making cappuccino (the steaming sputtering Italian espresso machine) Andrew thinks: if you had to be in the mood for somebody, if they had to be right for you every time, then all of us would end up lonely. Being with them is a good thing. Making dinner, having other voices in his little house, the squirrel sounds of Ray watching college football with the sound turned down, Elizabeth looking through his books. Just hanging out, the rough approximations of friendship.

The thing is, he feels this like a man going away, looking out the window of a train, watching the city slip away, knowing that he won't be back. . . .

Andrew's in a strange mood, now. He feels the same about everything, going, gone. Ray switches to beer. Andrew opens another bottle of wine. They talk: D.C. politics, gossip, real estate, nothing new. Nobody's going to tell him a thing but that's all right. They're here. He's not alone. It's another small victory, a world which seems to be turning faster and faster, flinging people off in all directions, and unless they manage to hold on to each other they are flung off alone and here, in this room, in this circle of candlelight and television light and lamplight, they are holding on to each other. They are still holding on. That's worth something.

"We've got to rescue the sitter," Elizabeth says at the stroke of eleven o'clock.

"No," says Andrew. "That's all right. I know my company isn't worth the five bucks an hour."

"I'd go as high as seven-fifty," Mark says, "but Mindy's, like, the high school girl down the street."

"Mandy," Elizabeth says.

"We'll be in desperate trouble with her parents if we don't get her home on time."

"Actually, I think she's got a party to go to," Elizabeth says.

"I remember when parties started at midnight," Ray says.

"Some of them still do," Andrew says. This all feels horribly false to him, false and self-important, but still he doesn't want them to go.

"I bet there are parties starting even now, with persons of our age and station, within a few short blocks of here," Andrew says. "I bet there are people drinking and taking drugs and enjoying themselves."

"What about Susan?" Mark asks.

"I'll get her up," says Ray.

"No, don't," says Elizabeth. "After a day like today."

"She can't stay here," Ray says.

"Sure she can," Andrew says. "I can camp out on the sofa. It's no problem at all."

"Let's see if she's even asleep," says Ray, and they all troop over to the bedroom door, it feels to Andrew like the apartment might list to that side with all the weight there, and Elizabeth gently turns the handle, silently, and there in the room—the lamp still lit—is Susan, warm and sleeping. Her cheeks are pink in the heat, her legs spread underneath her dress, careless. Beautiful, Andrew thinks. Sleeping beauty.

They all look, and then they draw back from the doorway, and Elizabeth—gently, motherly—slips the door shut again.

"She looks all right," Elizabeth says.

"I should take her home," Ray says.

"No," Mark says. "Let her sleep."

"It's fine," Andrew says. "I can give her a ride in the morning. It's no problem at all."

"The thing is," Mark says, "you have to wake her up every two hours, that's what the doctor said. If she's hard to wake up or if she gets a headache—anything severe—or if there's any nausea or vomiting, she needs to go to the emergency room right away. OK?"

"You were with her?" Andrew says.

Mark looks suddenly confused, embarrassed.

"I wasn't around," Ray says. "Mark was the one who had to pick her up."

"That was lucky," Andrew says. "Lucky you were around."

None of them will look at him. He's somewhere close but he can't tell where, where the trouble is. And part of him cares but part of him doesn't.

"I can take care of her," Andrew says. "It's no problem at all."

Ray still doesn't like the idea but he puts his coat on anyway, follows Elizabeth to the door, handshakes and kisses, Andrew doesn't want them to go but now that they're going he wants them out. A nice clean cut.

"Don't forget to wake her up," says Mark. "Every two hours."

And that's that.

The party debris, glasses and cups and empty bottles, the wineglass with Elizabeth's lipstick on the rim, Andrew gathers and straightens. It's good, this little mess—it takes away some of the newness of the apartment, some of the shine. It makes it feel almost like someone lives here, almost like home. Elizabeth, before she left, had stacked the dirty dishes next to the sink, had run a damp cloth over the new oak table. Andrew is just running the hot water into his sink when in walks Susan.

"They finally left," Susan says.

"You're awake," Andrew—the idiot—says.

"I thought they'd never leave."

"Did you sleep at all?"

"Ray's fucking Elizabeth," she says. "I just needed a night off."

She sits at the breakfast bar, selects the cleanest of the dirty wineglasses and pours the dregs of the red wine into it, a solid half a glass. Andrew is suddenly angry at her, at all of them. All the fucking marrieds, he thinks, all the stupid secrets, all the carelessness.

"Since when?" he says.

"Since forever," she says, "since always, since before you and before me and before all of it. They never stopped."

He feels it then, the big black certainty descending into his heart. He didn't matter even then. Didn't exist.

"Why?" he says, and Susan laughs.

"Because they want to," she says. "Because they can."

Andrew turns the water off. Why does this matter so much to him? But it does, he can feel it. Everybody knew but Andrew. Everybody was in on the joke.

Andrew goes to the little drawer next to the sink and takes out the pack of Camel Lights, the ashtray—his mother's ashtray—and the little plastic lighter, pours himself a glass of wine and goes into the dining room, trailing Susan.

"I didn't know you smoked," Susan says.

"This is what bothers me," he says, lighting a cigarette, pushing the pack toward her. "I go to sleep alone, not every night but a lot of nights. I think about children all the time, I mean I don't know, maybe it's just a fantasy of mine but I think about it. It's like there's some gene for making that connection, something that you've got and I don't. It doesn't matter what you do if you've got the gene. I mean Ray and Elizabeth, Jesus Christ. The world's oldest teenagers."

"I don't think it's like that," Susan says quietly. "I think it's a matter of finding the right person."

Jude bought this pack of cigarettes, he thinks. Jude for whom I also don't exist.

"Why do you put up with it?"

"I don't," she says. "Every time it happens is the last time. Then it happens again."

She shakes a cigarette out of the pack and holds it between her fingers, experimentally, taking a little imaginary puff.

"I wouldn't enjoy this, would I?"

"Probably not."

"Probably not," she says, and slips the cigarette back into

the pack. "So many things are like that, you think they must be really good because they're bad for you and then you try them and they're really not so good at all."

Small-voiced, careful, tucking the pack closed again with her hands and then looking at her hands. The quiet all around them, eleven-thirty. Andrew feels her confusion, finds an answering confusion in himself. What will she do next?

"I'm sorry to dump you in the middle of this," Susan says. "Sorry for all of it."

"What will you do now?"

"I don't know," she says, and looks up at him—and she doesn't know, doesn't even know where to start. Again he sees her, just for a moment, clearly, what it must feel like for her. Sees her driving down the street, toward them or away from them.

"Probably nothing," Susan says. "The same as ever. It doesn't feel like it, though."

"What?"

"I don't know," she says, and shakes her head. "I feel like I've played a trick on you, staying like this. I can call him."

"No."

"He's got the cell phone in his car."

"No, don't," he says—then feels like he said something he didn't mean to, gave himself away. He starts again: "I mean, you're more than welcome to stay. I'm not angry with you."

"You should be."

"OK, I am," he says. "Not really at you but at all of you. You should have taken better care."

"You're right," she says. "You're right."

Andrew stubs the cigarette out, sips his wine.

There she is, looking off into the corner, considering. Again he has the feeling of seeing her for the first time and maybe the last, the familiar version of her falling away and this new, unexpected person in her place.

Her hand on the table between them, open.

Andrew covers it with his own hand, then feels her take it in, curling around him, a blind turning toward the light. Takes his hand and raises it to her lips and kisses, first the palm, then the inside of his wrist. He feels her there with his whole body, a sharp galvanic burst of feeling, body-feeling and also the other, the surprise, the thing that had been there all evening. Susan.

And for the moment, be knows exactly what to do. He stands and draws her up to him and they embrace, like before but exactly different, they embrace as lovers, he feels her lips against his neck and sees Jude disappearing, going, gone, Mark and Elizabeth, little parts of himself, his past, all going, the little apartment, the little place for one where he was going to spend the rest of his life alone, he'll have to sell it now to make room for her but now she's here.

"How did I miss you?" Andrew says.

She shakes her head against his chest. "Don't talk," she says.

The Birthday Girl

SATURDAY NIGHT AT THE SIP 'N' DIP: PIANO
Pat is bellowing out her 35,000th rendition of "Take Me
Home, Country Roads" while the college boys and girls—home
for Christmas, stuck in town till New Year's—suck mixed
drinks off the piano-top bar and sing along. It's ten o'clock
or ten-thirty and the snow is coming down like a freight train
outside. I get a Daniel's ditch to go and take it back to the
room, not without regret. The bar is snug and warm and win-
dowless and loud. The street outside looks like the Ice Planet.

"Where's my Coke?" asks Justin.

"What Coke?"

"The one you didn't get me," he says.

I dig a wad of dollar bills out of the front pocket of my
jeans, separate one from the mass of change and throw it at

his head. Reflexively his hand comes up to catch it. He plays second base for his high school team in San Diego and is already platooning as a sophomore. When he gets up to go find the Coke machine, he is taller than me, again, as he has been this whole visit, which I find surprising, again.

I fire up the laptop and his mother's flight is still delayed, hasn't left Salt Lake, no arrival time specified. I'm glad I'm not there with her. She's easily bored and she gets frantic when she feels trapped, like a terrier in a box. Plus she doesn't smoke anymore, according to Justin, which would only make it worse. I remember her in that exact airport, remember looking at her in the glassed-in smoking room, talking and smiling with her fellow sinners while the rest of us sat alone and bored. On the television, the Dallas Cowboy cheerleaders are taking on the beautiful Raiderettes in a tug-of-war across a mud pit, under a blue, blue sky and the flickering shade of palm trees. It's some kind of danger, but fun danger—with mud-wrestling overtones—and the girls all have big white smiles. They're having a terrific time. Outside the motel room, the wind whistles in the corners of the building, and snow taps against the glass.

"We've got a cleaning lady," Justin says. "Beat that."

He flops onto the bed, at length and at speed, and the bed complains.

"I've got a girl comes in once in a while," I tell him. "She's supposed to come tomorrow. When it's just me, I don't need the help."

"You're saying I'm a mess?"

"Hell, yes, I am. Do you ever look behind you?"

"No."

"Well, you ought to," I tell him. "A trail of empty soda cans and candy wrappers and dirty socks and I don't know what-all else."

"Granny," he says.

"Pigboy," I tell him.

I snap the silver Apple shut and go look out the window, at the horizontal snow flying through the streetlight, the cars inching down the street, the cones of their headlights outlined in snow. Elaine will never make it down in this weather, or even up, if she's lucky. Better to cancel the flight completely than to spend those hours circling, waiting for the weather to break, a slot to land in. I picture Elaine in her own motel room, alone and eight hundred miles away; and I'll admit I do take a certain satisfaction in this image. Let her suffer for once. Let her spend the night alone.

Justin watches the cheerleaders while I call up to the Black Star to see how things are going with the storm. Carter tells me everything's buttoned up tight and the cattle are down in the draws where they ought to be. He says it's not snowing that hard up there and he doesn't even think it'll get down to zero. I tell him I'm definitely stuck for the night and some hard-to-figure chunk of the next day. Originally Justin and his mom were supposed to fly out at ten the next morning but all bets are off in this weather.

I summarize what Carter told me in a short e-mail and

send it off to New York. I manage the Black Star for a person you have seen on television. It's really more of a desk job than you might think but I still look OK on a horse.

"They're getting married," Justin says.

This takes a moment to sink in. When it does. I wonder why he's been here for ten days and only now decided to tell me. I ask him exactly that.

"I don't know," Justin says. He keeps his eyes careful on the TV, where the cheerleaders are trying to balance on big rubber balls, like six feet tall. He says, "I just thought you wouldn't like it much. Plus I thought Mom ought to be the one to tell you."

"Is that why she was coming to pick you up?"

Justin shrugs, but I know I'm right, and I know I should have seen it coming months ago, when this plan started. It didn't make sense even then. Fifteen years old, he could fly on his own, as he did on the way up. I knew this all along. I hoped all along that she wanted to talk, though I didn't know about what. Something to say to me. Not this.

Justin says, "I just don't think she's going to make it in tonight."

"No, you're right."

"I bet I end up meeting her in Salt Lake tomorrow."

"When's the wedding?"

"June," he says.

"At the Coronado."

"Good guess."

"It wasn't a guess," I tell him. "She's wanted to get married at a place like that her whole life. She likes it fancy. I guess Del can afford fancy."

"Oh, yeah."

Outside is wild wind and windblown snow. Eleven o'clock on a Saturday night and there's nobody on the street, nobody, not a car and not a walker—except, now that I look, a single old man in a red-and-black plaid jacket is making his way into the wind, inching forward under the brim of his hat. He walks slowly and with determination. I am suddenly and for no good reason heartbroken to look at him. Alone and out in the weather, on a night when nobody ought to be out. Really, I know he's probably just another mean drunk, walking home from the bar because he's got too many DUIs to drive anymore. But looking at him, alone and small, I find something giving way inside me.

When I turn back from the window, I catch Justin studying me. He whips his eyes back to the TV but too late. I can see he's been watching, trying to see how I'll react to his little bit of news. Not that there's anything wrong with that. Of course he's curious.

"You can go down to the bar if you want," he says. "I'm just going to watch TV for a while. I can come get you if she calls or something."

I don't say anything.

"I'm fine," he says.

This night is Justin's last till spring, and I know I should stay. But he's been here long enough this time to see inside me, and what I feel right now is not anything a father wants his son to see, small and weak and helpless. Elaine is getting married. Of course she's getting married! It's no business of mine. But I do feel completely undermined by the news.

"Maybe just one drink," I tell him. "Just a quick one. I'm pretty sure she won't make it in."

"A hundred percent positive," he says. "Do they really have mermaids?"

"Sure they do."

"You've seen them?"

"I've seen pictures."

"But you've never seen an actual mermaid?"

"Not yet," I tell him. "One of these days."

"Come get me if you see one tonight, OK?" he says. "I mean it. The minute the mermaids come out, you come get me."

"Will do," I say. "They weren't out before, though. But I'll definitely get you if they show."

"Definitely," he says.

The Sip 'n' Dip Lounge, you see, is on the second floor of the motel, and the pool is on the third floor, and the whole back of the bar is a big window into the underwater part of the pool. I'm not kidding. You can look this up. Some nights they have a show, where girls in bathing suits and mermaid flippers do artistic underwater dances while breathing out of air hoses. I've seen the pictures, and I've had it described to me. All the way down the long hallways of the motel, I hope that they'll be out when I get to the bar. It seems like a fine night for mermaids.

When I get to the bar, though, the pool is almost empty and things have slowed down from before. The college students have taken their fun somewhere else, Piano Pat has gone on break, or maybe gone for the night—it's eleven-thirty already, which kind of snuck up on me. A light tinkly jazz is playing way in the background, and the couples that remain are scattered among the booths, the fishing nets and tiki faces and plaster-of-paris octopi. Instead of mermaids, we have a hefty couple in the pool behind the bar.

I order a Daniel's on the rocks and a bottle of Bud, which is what I order when I want to get a buzz on. I could have stayed married if I had wanted to. She was the one who left but I was the one who made the thing impossible. I knew that. Still, I loved her. Not that I had any high hopes or expectations, I wasn't waiting, wasn't holding my breath. But just the idea that she's going to be married—and not just married but married to Del, who lives in a gated community and sends out newsletters about himself three times a year—I feel like I'm about to let go of something I didn't know I was holding on to. *No affection*, she wrote. Justin showed me one of the newsletters once, full of interesting information about Del, illustrated with full-color glossy pictures.

"It's my birthday today," says the woman on the next bar stool.

"Well," I say. "Happy birthday to you."

In the dim light, she looks incredibly wholesome, long light-brown hair drawn back into a wide clip at the back of her neck, a flowered blouse and a long dark skirt. On the bar in front of her sits a brown beer bottle with the label scratched off almost entirely. Little shreds of label paper line the bar in front of her like mouse turds.

"I'm supposed to be in Mexico right now," she says.

I leave this alone for a minute and the both of us sip our drinks and watch the underwater couple, back behind the bar. The magnifying effect of the water makes their legs look huge, like manatees. They might know we're watching but they might not. In the blue light, their giant legs twine together. God knows what their upper halves are doing but their legs can't seem to stop touching.

"I haven't been sexual for a long time," says the woman.

She stops there, and waits for a response, but I can't think of one. After a minute she says, "It was never really a priority for me, and then I went on the antidepressants. I'll tell you, that whole first wave, Prozac, Wellbutrin, those things would really knock you for a loop in that department. You ever get tangled up with that stuff?"

"Not me."

"No, of course not," she says. "Every woman I know over thirty is on antidepressants, every damn one. The men just drink themselves into the bag every night. That's why the Spanish and the Koreans and all are taking this country over, ten o'clock comes around and the guys are three sheets to the wind and the ladies are, like, wood from the waist down. Do me a favor."

"Anything," I tell her. I mean it.

"I'm going to buy a pack of cigarettes here in a minute,"

she says, "but when you go, I want you to take them with you. Toss them out, run them under the sink, I don't care. Just get them out of my sight. Otherwise I'll smoke the whole pack and then I'll smell like cigarettes for Bob."

"Bob."

"My fiancé," she says. "Down in Puerto Vallarta."

"Everybody's getting married," I tell her.

"Not quite everybody," she says. She lifts herself off the bar stool with a light, undrunken grace and goes out into the hallway, where the vending machines and restrooms are. If she isn't drunk, then what? I think about Justin, back in the room, and think that maybe I should just slip out while she's gone. I don't, though. I order another Daniel's on the rocks and settle back and watch the giant manatee legs afloat in the blue, fake-looking water. The light at this end of the bar is mainly from the swimming pool and filtered blue. The legs seem very friendly with each other. A hand floats down briefly into the water, then gone again into the air.

"You want to hear something strange?"

It's the girl again, or the woman, whatever—somewhere around thirty, plus or minus, with a sweet concerned face and wholesome hair. She shakes a Marlboro out of the pack, then offers me one, which I take.

"What's your name?" I ask her.

"My twin sister's birthday was yesterday," she says. "I bet you can't explain that."

"She was born at 11:59 and you were born at 12:01," I tell her.

She looks crestfallen for a moment, then perks back up. She says, "I hear they have mermaids."

"Not tonight," says the bartender, a stout redheaded woman with a face like the prow of a ship. She says, "Everything's buttoned up tonight with the snow and all. The mermaids called in at eight o'clock and said they weren't even going to try. I'll be lucky to make it home myself."

"Try Mexico," says the girl on the next stool. "Try getting to Puerto Vallarta in this."

"Do you have a dog?" I ask her.

"Why?"

"It seems like you've got one of everything else. One twin sister, one fiancé."

"One leg," she says, and giggles.

"Really?"

"You'll never know," she says. "It's one more item in the vast unknowable universe, one more piece of information beyond your ken."

"I would like to buy you a drink in honor of your birthday," I say.

"Gwen," she says. "And you?"

"Richard."

"Richard, I would love a piña colada."

"Done and done," I tell her. The bartender has overheard, and with invisible bartender gestures asks if I would like another drink, too, and I imperceptibly nod *yes.* Gwen places on the bar in front of us a photograph of a very large and mournful-looking dog, some sort of mastiff, mostly white, with a single large brown spot on his side. He's lying on his side on a wooden porch and in the background is lush, dense, green forest, almost a jungle, like nothing around here.

"Where are you from, anyway?" I ask.

She doesn't say anything, just takes my arm in her firm grip and I follow her eyes upward to the tank. The bartender brings the drinks, makes change out of the twenty I left on the bar, then she looks up into the tank as well. The hand has returned. It's a woman's hand with a wedding ring and we all watch it disappear down the back of the man's bathing trunks.

"Oh, for Christ's sake," says the bartender, and turns to a faithful customer at the end of the bar. "Wayne? Wayne, would you go tell those people that everybody is watching."

"Sure thing," says Wayne. "Right now?"

"This is not going to end well," says the bartender.

Gwen is staring up into the blue light of the tank, as if she's seeing something more than the rest of us, which maybe she is. Nothing really seems to be happening. It's just a hand resting on somebody's ass, and watching it makes me lonely. His legs are all right, hairy and muscular, but her legs seem like an example of all the flab and rot and death that comes to the body. The woman these legs belong to is not young and not tall and not slim. And yet they are there together, touching, floating in the pool. They think they're alone. They forgive each other enough to touch. They float.

"The things that I want and the things that I need, I can't get them to match up," Gwen says, still watching intently. "The people that I love. Bob tells me I smell like cigarettes."

"It's your birthday," I tell her. "You can have a little fun."

"It's my *birthday*? Who told you that?"

"You did."

Her eyes slowly peel from the blue water of the tank and down to my arm, which her hand is still gripping. I had forgotten this myself. Her eyes open wide as she takes her hand away, and her mouth twists into sorrow.

"My god," she says. "I was saying those things out loud. I was talking, wasn't I?"

"A little," I tell her.

"All that time, I thought I was dreaming," she says. She suddenly looks deflated, quite drunk, and the bartender is staring at me as if I made it happen. She was here first but that's not going to matter. I think of Justin, back in the room, and know that I have made a mistake by coming here. I think of the snow outside. Gwen says, "The pills."

"You'd better go back to your room," says the bartender.

Gwen says, "I can't remember which one is mine."

"It's on your key. See if you can find your key."

Just then the light goes strange and wavy and when I look up, the couple are scrambling out of the pool and the surface of the water, reflecting down at us, is in a turmoil. The light is agitated on Gwen's face as she dumps the contents of her bag on the bar in front of her—change, mints, pens and Kleenex, a PalmPilot and a cell phone—then rakes through them with her fingers, finding pennies. Finding an aerosol of Mace, which the bartender shouldn't ought to see. I nudge it back into her purse and there is her key, right in front of her, room 212.

"Thank you, Richard," she says. "There's something wrong with me."

"Do you want me to help you find your room?"

"Yes," she says.

The bartender scowls at me—she disapproves of picking off the drunk—but I'm an innocent man, my intentions are good, I mean to walk her to the room and come right back! Or maybe just go back to the room, keep Justin company if he's still awake, which he is. The boy doesn't sleep, except all morning long. Gwen gathers her things back into her bag and steps gingerly off the bar stool, a little fun-house wobble in her move. She was fine a minute ago. Piano Pat is firing up the Wurlitzer as we leave, a flurry of arpeggios that gradually resolves into "Bad, Bad Leroy Brown."

"I'm not going to fuck you," Gwen says in the hallway.

A college boy, out to get ice and fifty feet ahead of us, is surprised to hear it. He turns and stares.

"I didn't think you were," I tell her. The hallway stretches far in front of us, ending at a blind corner; the parking lot, through the glass doors, is filling up with snow like milk in a glass. The cars are unrecognizable mounds, animal-like shapes, like white cats curled up to sleep. The college boy waits by the ice machine, waits till we pass and eyes us eagerly. He's curious. I fight the urge to flip him off. Piano Pat's music—drum machine, piano, synthesizer, organ—echoes and pursues us down the long hallway, like a poisonous fog.

We get to room 212 in what feels like half an hour. I hand her the key, which I have been holding for her, and say something mild and polite by way of good-bye, feeling faintly relieved.

"Wait," says Gwen.

"Wait for what?"

"I don't want to be alone," she says. "Just for a minute. Come on."

She turns the key and slowly opens the door and holds it open for me to walk through. And look, I know what you're thinking, but it isn't that. I don't expect to do anything with her. I don't even want to go in. But her face just looks so lost and lonely, so momentarily *naked*, it would be a betrayal to turn away. I've looked like that before, I think. When Elaine first left, I did. I couldn't just turn my back.

Inside her room is not what I was expecting.

The flowers, for one thing, a round array of pink and purple and green poking out of the ice bucket, a single red carnation in a water glass by the bed, a couple of snapdragon- or orchid-looking things on the other bedside table. The air of the room is still and full with the smell of flowers, and of her products and perfumes, a little stale. Also, there are candles, which she had apparently left burning on the desk by the TV while she went to the bar. On the table sits a still life of wine and bread and cheese, a lonely dinner. In the corner, by the closet, sits a set of black professional luggage, the frequent flyer's Travelpro Rollaboard and the big black sample case.

She lies down upon the bed and starts to weep. I stand in the doorway, uncertain. Where should I put myself? I never know what to do with a crying woman. I never seem to meet any other kind. Gwen has curled herself into the shape of an S, her face turned away from me. I don't know what to do with my body. Once more, it seems to me that I should just go, back to my son, back to my life. I remember, just at that moment, nursing baby Justin through a bout of croup on a cold winter night, a night he couldn't catch his breath and the three of us alone in a place so far from anywhere that we couldn't see a ranch light from our porch, nothing but stars. And here he was, he couldn't breathe, two years old or even less. And I remember taking him into the shower, and holding him in the steam, trying not to drop him, the slippery-smooth little body. And after a while he started to sound OK. We stayed an hour longer in the steam, just to make sure, and all that time Elaine was on the porch, smoking cigarettes and praying. I don't know why this comes to me but it does: the soft wet skin, the panic.

"You shouldn't leave candles burning when you're not here," I tell her, when the tears stop. "You could burn the place down."

"It's fireproof," she says.

"You're not."

"No," says Gwen. "But I don't care."

She smiles at me after she says this, a bright artificial grin that shuts off quickly as a lightbulb. Like an old woman, she gets out of bed slowly, stiffly, and sits at the table and pours a glass of wine for herself out of an open bottle, then one for me. She's thinking. She still looks wholesome, whole wheat, like the kind of girl who might have made her outfit herself, all long brown straight glossy hair, neat as a pin. I lie down on a bed for five minutes these days and I get up looking like I've been dead for a week. She, on the other hand, looks fresh and clean.

"You need somebody to take care of you," I tell her.

"I know."

"It's not going to be me."

"I never thought it was," she says. "It's not going to be Bob, either. Sitting on a beach in Mexico."

"He changed his mind."

"Nope," Gwen says. "He just stopped answering his cell phone."

"Maybe his battery went dead."

"Maybe."

"Maybe Bob is dead."

"I hope so," she says—then shudders, like she has said something unlucky. "I don't want him dead," she says. "I just want him to suffer a little."

"You should introduce him to my ex-wife," I tell her.

"Ha, ha," she says. "Just like Jay Leno."

I sit across from her at the table and I take her hand in mine and look at it, touch it: a girl's hand, soft and long-fingered, with pointed, painted nails. She is, to this extent, taking care of herself. I don't look at her face. I don't really want to know what's in it, what expectation or what fear. I just focus on her small, soft, attractive hand between my own.

I tell her, "When it's gone, it's gone. You'll know. You should go to him when the weather breaks."

"What if he's not there? What if he doesn't want to see me?"

"You'll be alone," I say. "Same as now but with palm trees and sunshine."

"I mean to do well," she says—and when I look up, she's staring into my face, like she means to be understood, like this is somehow suddenly important. She says, "I try to do the right thing but I feel like I'm always, I don't know, things are running away from me. Like I got off the SSRIs so I could, you know, be with Bob. Be enthusiastic, because, you know, people like that in a person. Enthusiasm. But then, I don't know, it's like everything speeded up and got all edgy, like when I quit smoking the first time, that little voice that wouldn't shut up saying *time for a cigarette, time for a cigarette*. . . . You know? Like nothing would stay where it was supposed to be, nothing was at rest. So I take these other things just to slow things down and meanwhile Bob won't have anything to do with me. He says my *personality* is suddenly a problem and it's just because I'm trying to make him happy. Nothing ever works out the way I planned it. Do you think I'm pretty?"

"I do," I tell her, and rub the warm skin of the back of her hand.

She stands, and in one gesture, it feels like, steps free of her plain skirt and blouse, discards her bra and then stands naked before me in only her knee socks, never taking her eyes off my face. Her body is perfect. There's something blinding about it, too bright to be stared at directly, there in the pale candlelight—and the searchlights of her eyes, playing over my face, looking for something, looking for what?

Whatever is wrong with her, it is nothing I can fix, or even help. I know this all at once. It's a mistake for me to be here.

"Do you think I'm beautiful?" she asks.

Because she is, she knows it, she's beautiful but she's dead, and I feel myself drawn toward her, toward the taste of ashes in my mouth. I rise to leave, but I don't leave. I can't seem to. Like gravity, she pulls me in. Her body is perfect, full as a ripe fruit. Her pubic hair is pale gold, honey-colored.

Then I remember Justin, back in the room—his little body, wet with soap, so many years ago—alone in our room, and I know I shouldn't be here, I know I don't want him to end up this way, alone.

"I'm sorry, I'm sorry, I'm sorry," I tell her. "I have to go."

"Don't go," she says.

"I have to."

"Not tonight," she says. "It's just one night."

"I have to go," I tell her. And even then, it's half a slow minute longer before I can gather myself to go, take my eyes from hers, turn my back on her lovely body and automatically walk away, out the door and into the hallway and down the hallway, breaking through sticky little cobwebs of need and desire, half mistaken, ready to turn back or to flee, at the same time. I feel like I've been narrowly rescued, at the same time wanting to turn back to her, wanting not so much to touch her—though I do want to touch her—as to help, if I can, for just one night, her loneliness.

I stand at the doorway to the parking lot and press my

hot forehead against the cold glass. Outside the wind has died down but the snow has continued to fall, big fat flakes drifting slowly down, slowly as the snow in one of those Christmas balls filled with slow liquid, the little house with the snowman out front....

Elaine is waiting for me when I get back to the room, Elaine and Justin.

Immediately I feel accused, and I am—she can smell it on me, the perfume, candle smoke and cigarettes. She always could.

"What are you doing here?" I ask her.

She looks good, stylish, expensive, sleek. She air-kisses me on either cheek and gives me a guarded, warning look. We're not going to talk about it with Justin around.

"They landed us in Helena and bused us up," she says. "A hellish drive."

"I was just down in the bar," I tell her.

"Really?" Elaine says. "I was just looking for you there. Just a few minutes ago."

"You must have just missed me."

"I'm sure I did," she says.

And this is all. In a minute, she will go back to her room down the hall; in six hours, we'll all be awake again, and I'll be driving back to the airport in the snow, the bright sunshine painful on the white, white snow. In a couple of days you'll be back playing second base under the rustling palm trees, and I know that you'll be wondering what happened on this night, and I think someday I might tell you, though I can't imagine where or when it would come up. Just another day in the river of days, long gone.

And this last thing: I went back, the night after you left. I don't know if I was looking for her exactly but I did check to see if she was still at the hotel. Of course she was long gone. But I went back down to the bar, just to have a drink anyway, and that night the mermaids were out. And this was the thing, I knew one of them—she was this girl I met when I was talking to a class at the Vo-Tech, talking about range management. Just a pretty girl, an ag major. But then I looked up through the glass and I saw her and I recognized her right away, even with her hair all floating around her face and her feet bound up into a rubber fin. And this is the thing that's amazing to me, I never realized this but I guess they can see back through the glass and into the bar, because she recognized me, too. She swam up to the glass and she smiled at me and waved, and I waved back, and then she breathed in, from her air hose, and out again. A string of bubbles drifted out of her mouth and up through the lit blue water and out, into the unseen sky above the surface.

The Boreal Forest

A MARRIAGE, ANY MARRIAGE but your own, is
one thing you will never know. The faith that binds two people
together, the doubts that separate us, the conversations and
the silences—all happen in private, out of anybody's light but
our own. Are we happy? Do we even like each other? It's like
the dark side of the moon, the face that's turned away from
you. And even when a marriage is over, when the ex-husband
or ex-wife sits you down to tell what it was really like, the story
is all hopelessly false. A marriage is alive for as long as it's alive,
and then it's gone. What's left is no more than a bitter smell,
like something burning. It fills the empty space where the feeling used to be. But it is not the feeling.

So: in a bed, in a house, in the night, in the dense and
dripping afterwards of an autumn rain, Catherine and I lay
reading, side by side. This was October. Our daughter, El-

lie, twelve, was pretending sleep upstairs. We had bought an upstairs-and-downstairs house after she was born, to save a little privacy for ourselves, but twelve years later we still slept in pajamas—the touch of a familiar body through T-shirt cotton—while Ellie did anything she wanted to upstairs.

Catherine read her book-club book; it might have been Naguib Mahfouz that week, or *The God of Animals*. I was reading Helen and Scott Nearing, old Communists and backwoods pioneers, about hand-laying stone walls. We had bought some dirt in the mountains north of us, a little patch of ground with a pond and an old quarry, and I was going to build us a cabin on it. Actually, by then we had owned the land for three or maybe even four years and had done nothing but camp on it a couple of times. When we had bought it—mainly my idea— Ellie was smaller, and I imagined her as some little pioneer girl, handing her father a stone and admiring him as he laid it precisely into the wall. She was never anything like that. Once in a while we talked about selling it but it was easier to continue to think that someday it might happen. There was no hurry. We had plenty of money.

Catherine was drinking mint tea and I was drinking some dark fancy beer she had bought and we were fading toward sleep. Just then, I remembered something I had heard at work that day. I said, Peter and Maria are splitting up.

She startled—I could feel it—like the news came physically to her. We had been touching incidentally but she drew away.

Where did you hear this?

I can't remember, I said. It's true, though. Sarah saw Maria in the Good Food store and she told her.

I felt her pull away, into the intimate cool distance. I sipped my beer.

What happened? she said after a minute. Does anybody know what happened?

I don't know, I said. Maybe nothing happened.

You're no good for anything at all, she said. And though I knew she meant it as a joke, she was a little more emphatic than she needed to be, something in her tone of voice that I recognized, a sharpness that scared me off. Here's something to not think about, I thought. Here's something I don't want to know.

Crazy, she said after a minute.

But she whispered it to someone else, someone other than me, not in the room.

Crazy, I said, and shut my light off and rolled onto my side. I had to be up at quarter to five, and it was probably nothing. I lay there facing away from her for a long time, waiting for sleep to come and then, after a while, pretending that it had. A long time after I had shut off the light, forty-five minutes at least, Catherine bent toward me and kissed my shoulder and whispered, quiet so as not to wake me up, I love you.

* * *

I got up to Elvis Presley singing "Cold Kentucky Rain" and took a shower while the coffee was brewing and filled my thermos and left, left my little house of sleeping women. Had I slept at all? Everything felt like an alias of itself.

I had packed the pickup truck the afternoon before and I was on the interstate before daybreak, following my headlights, sipping my coffee, listening to the intermittent slap of the wipers. It wasn't raining hard. It would be snowing up on the pass, where I was going. Between my dreams and my dark waking life and my thoughts of the high country I was going into— the first snow drifting down through the dark fir trees, the smell of ice—I felt floaty and insubstantial, and I made myself focus on the trip at hand, a way to tie myself down. I was going up into the Great Burn to look for lynx, which I would not see. Nobody ever sees lynx. My colleague Rick Johnson has been working the mountains behind Seeley Lake for thirty years, way back into the wilderness, and he has never seen one. I have never seen one. I have seen tracks, have combed their fur out of traps and sent it off for DNA analysis, have even, on one occasion, even smelled one, I think, though there's no way of knowing for sure. But I have never seen one.

These days we leave the fieldwork to the graduate students. This trip of mine was an exception, a reward for a summer spent in the office, crunching numbers and working on grants. I have to get out once in a while. Otherwise I go all stale and housebound. I felt self-contained and self-reliant, with my sleeping bag and cooler snug in the back of my truck, three days alone in open country ahead of me. I was going into the boreal forest, the high country, the only place a wild lynx can live, the last stop before timberline—and above timberline, too, a green rocky park of cliffs and lakes and glacial cirques. I had been in the area before but south of where I was going. This country would all be new to me.

I remembered as I drove past Tarkio that I had seen Maria in my dreams the night before. Had I kissed her? It wouldn't have been the first time. I had known her for as long as I knew Catherine—they were roommates when we met, friends, always, afterward. The first night Catherine and I slept together, Maria slept in the next room. For the first ten years of our marriage she was the unofficial third partner, friend, witness and referee. Friday nights on the sofa, watching old movies and eating pizza. She was even present in the delivery room when Ellie was born, holding Catherine's other hand. But four years ago she met Peter.

I pulled off the highway at Superior, gassed up at the Town Pump and bought a twelve-pack for the cooler. The dawn was breaking blue through the clouds and the rain was turning to mud. I left the pavement behind and switched on my GPS as I started up toward the pass.

And yes, it did seem strange that Catherine didn't know about the split, that she had to find out from me. But they hadn't been close for a long time, she and Maria. There was a falling away after the marriage, which was only natural. Also Peter was one of my graduate students at the time—we introduced them to each other—but not one of my best, in the end. Others did better, went on to teaching jobs. Peter was still doing seasonal work for one or the other of the consulting firms around town. We never talked about it but I know he felt that

I could have done more for him. Plus they were tied to the area because of Maria's job, so he really couldn't look elsewhere. It had been a year or two since the four of us met for dinner. But Catherine still met Maria for coffee or drinks once in a while. Didn't she?

I turned off the main road and the driving began to need my attention. I got out in the rain, turned the hubs, put it in four-wheel and spread the forest map on the seat next to me. Between me and where I was trying to get to was a spider-web of jammer roads to untangle. There was logging going on someplace ahead, too; a paper plate nailed to a tree at the turnoff said CB 9 in orange paint and I turned my radio to that channel to listen for log trucks. It was slow going, a narrow road and an uphill grind, second gear all the way. I remembered that I had kissed Maria in my dreams the night before, and maybe more than that. I'd seen her naked, a few times, though not for years. We used to go up to the hot springs, the three of us, and a couple of times with baby Ellie. She had a lush, beautiful body and a pleasant face. It was strange that she hadn't had better luck with men.

The road stayed back in the trees for most of the way but once in a while it came out onto a bald spot and I could see how high up I was. The ground dropped away sharply and there was the interstate below, looking like something you'd see out of a plane. It was a little dizzying, looking down like that, and mostly I kept my eyes on the road. Catherine says it's not falling that you're afraid of, it's jumping. I could just steer the wheel half a turn to the right . . . but I didn't, and after a while the road turned to face the backcountry, and all I saw below me was a blanket of evergreen, shading into the mist and cloud.

We did sleep together once, Maria and I, while the baby slept in the other room. Catherine was at her mother's funeral. We didn't mean to.

I don't think I'm any worse than anybody else, I'm sure of it, in fact.

It was snowing by the time I made it up to the turnaround, little needle drops of snow that fell down through the rain, but that was all right with me. It made everything look pretty, white and lacy on the green grass. I decided to stay in the truck that night, though, and not take my tent and sleeping bag in to the lake. I was prepared, either way. But if it dumped that night, I didn't want to get stuck slogging out through a foot of snow. I took my day pack, loaded it with spare socks and rain gear, salami, apples and cheese, a plastic Nalgene jug of water and a purifier to fill it again from the lake, some extra combs and sample bags for the lynx trap and a jar of dead and almost completely decomposed rabbit parts, the bait for the trap. The jar was tightly closed and wrapped in plastic and didn't smell like anything at all. But the sight of it brought back the memory of the smell, pungent, lingering and completely foul, and for a moment I was nauseated.

I laced my boots up tight and then stood around for a minute, trying to remember what I'd forgotten.

Gaiters, I decided. Just in case it really dumped. Actually I thought it would probably warm up and start to rain again but I wanted to be careful.

The first couple of miles of the trip in were easy, following the Forest Service trail up along the ridgeline. After half an hour I was out of the trees and into an alpine meadow; I couldn't see it in the clouds and snow but I could feel it around me. If the weather ever broke, there would be hundred-mile views into Idaho from here. Million-dollar views is what the real-estate people would call them. This was a feeling that I had sometimes in the woods, a feeling that I was rich, things that I saw and things that I touched that money couldn't buy: the larch trees turning gold in the fall, the taste of a wild strawberry.

I couldn't help feeling like there was some connection between that night with Maria and the breakup, though I knew there couldn't be. That night was years before they had even met. I guess Ellie wasn't really a baby by then but more of a toddler, sleeping through the night. It was a Friday night, a pizza-and-a-movie night. The funeral was to be the next day. I remember Catherine calling to ask if I'd invited Maria, and I said I hadn't, and she said I ought to. Maria had just gone through another of her breakups and Catherine didn't want her sitting around moping on a Friday night. It was a regular thing, these Friday nights, when Maria was between boyfriends.

I don't know which one of us started it. It was hot, and all the windows of the house were open. We sat sweating on the leather couch and waiting for the movie to end, while Ellie slept in the air-conditioning of the bedroom. We were watching some movie that Catherine had rented, I don't remember what it was called but it had a lot of underwater life, a lot of swimming and seaweed. We were both a little bored with it. I got up to go to the bathroom and to check on Ellie and when I came back, Maria was out on the patio, smoking under the Christmas lights. She was dressed for the heat in a tank top and jean shorts. I took the cigarette from her hand and took a drag from it, which was not a thing I would have done if Catherine had been there. I took it without asking.

You know how these things go.

I know what you're thinking, and maybe you're right. Maybe you would have done things differently, maybe better. You'll probably never know. But maybe you'll find yourself with a pretty, willing girl on a hot night, with nobody watching and nobody to get hurt, and then we'll both know for sure. Won't we?

Two miles in, I had a choice to make. The snow was coming thicker and faster, and though it wasn't getting any deeper on the ground, visibility was pretty much zero. The lynx trap—the first one on the circular route I had planned—lay in a little pocket of alpine fir, a couple of miles cross-country from the trail I was on. I didn't know the country. I was alone. It might have been a good idea to turn around.

I didn't, though—didn't want to. I'd been looking forward to this little trip for weeks. I had a set of GPS coordinates for the trap and I had set a waypoint for the truck, plus it was only nine in the morning. I had all day, and I knew I would have this day to myself. All alone in wild country, with a good pair of boots and a pack on my back and work to do: this was a luxury I didn't often get.

I set off cross-country, following the arrow on the screen of the GPS, trying to read the land around me from the twenty feet I could see. It was really socked in, a heavy, steady, dense snowfall. The trap was eight hundred feet or so above the trail, a steady climb but not a steep one, and the ground was slick with snow as it started to pile up. I nearly slipped in a couple of steep sections. Most of the ground around here was grass and dead flowers but some of it was rock outcrops, little cliffs, pools where the water would collect at their base. In the dim light and the falling snow, the cliffs and hollows were pretty, Japanese-looking, with trees of dead leaves hanging out over them.

Then the GPS went out. The screen went blank. I tried to turn it off again to see if I could turn it on but nothing happened.

No sweat, I thought. I had backup batteries in my pack.

But when I found them, unscrewed the back of the unit and replaced the batteries, nothing happened. It wouldn't turn on. This was unexpected. Not terrible but unexpected. It cast a whole new light on things.

I had been looking forward to this little trip for weeks and now it was over. I kept a running calculation in my mind—of how long it would take to get back to Superior for batteries, or even back to town if I needed a whole new unit, of the likelihood of getting back out here before nightfall—and there was no way to make sense of it. Back to my little office, to my little empty house. Ellie would be at school now, and Catherine at work. The quiet house, ten-thirty on a weekday. I used to work at home some days and I liked the freedom of it, padding around in my sweat pants. I could picture it in my mind.

I started down the hill, figuring that the route would be easy: pick up the ridge trail I had started from, then follow it back to the truck. Within a quarter mile—I had been quite close to the top when the GPS gave out—the snow was two or three inches deep, obliterating my footprints from the way up. Again, I thought, no problem, follow the terrain down. Just like water.

When I came to the drop-off, though, I had to stop. This was unexpected and unwelcome. I hadn't seen anything like it on the way up but I hadn't seen anything else, either, just my little moving bubble. It wasn't so steep that I couldn't scramble down, at least as far as I could see, but it would be a slippery bitch in this weather, and I wasn't sure how far down I had to go. It trailed off into the snow, like the rest of the world around me. The prudent thing would be to stop and double back, see if I could find the easier slope I had come up on. The prudent thing would have been to turn back when it started to snow like this. But it was a little late for that.

I followed my footsteps back up the hill until the snow erased them again.

I did not truly know that I was lost until I doubled across my own bootprints in the snow. I was going in circles. Even then I did not panic. The snow was coming thick and fast, true, and I could not see to find my way out. But it was still—I checked my watch—still only ten forty-five in the morning, I had food, extra clothing, there was time. Surely it would clear sometime that day, in time to walk out. I had checked the weather on the Internet the night before and it said nothing about a big storm.

Mountains make their own weather, though. Up high like this, there was no predicting anything.

I found a stand of fir trees and nestled down among the branches. Inside was dark and still, like a little room. The snow collected on the branches of the trees and inside was dry, even the duff on the forest floor was dry. I peeled my outer wool coat off and found that it weighed about fifteen pounds with all the snow that had melted into it; put on an extra sweater and a stocking cap, pulled the coat back on, bundled up as warm as toast. I am a traditionalist when it comes to outdoor clothing and a day like that one is why. My feet were warm and dry in leather boots that gleamed with mink oil. My stout wool coat and Malone pants would get me through this storm.

I couldn't get the song "Achy Breaky Heart" out of my head, though. I thought that I would die as I had lived, as a ridiculous man. I don't know why I thought that. I wasn't going to die there. I mean, it was certainly possible, but it was not the most likely thing. Most likely, my life would continue as it had before, a series of small unimportant mistakes. I thought of my cell phone, down in the center well of the pickup truck. I had not wanted to bring it because I disliked it so, and because it seemed so out of place in the wilderness. But cell coverage was often surprisingly good above timberline, weak signals from far away but enough to connect. It was all line of sight.

I dug into my pack and found cheese and crackers, a chub of Molinari wine salami and my jug of water, and I thought: the ridiculous man prepares his last meal. I don't know why I was letting myself go on like that. I wasn't going anywhere, at least not that day. I would certainly die but not on that mountain. I was warm and dry and the food was good from hours of walking to sharpen the appetite.

I could not turn the thought of my death away, though. If I looked out from my little sheltering ground, the snow would have obliterated every trace of my passing, as if I had never been there. And there was no one to listen, if I cried out for help. No human voice could hear me. And I could expect no help from God. The thing about sin—I know it's an old-fashioned word, and out of style; I'll use a better one, if you can find it—the whole action of sin is a turning away, it's part of the thrill. Not just turning away from God, I never really had much going with God anyway, never prayed to him except on mountain passes, during ice storms, Ellie's illnesses and other emergencies. I was a hypocrite, it's true.

Because, you know, it's really very hard to stop something like that once it starts, something like Maria. Even if we'd wanted to. There were interruptions, stops and starts. But something always drew us back together, some accident or intention, some sense of our always sharing this one big secret. We were the only ones who knew, and it was a big thing to know.

All through Ellie's growing up, all through the years, afternoons and evenings, sometimes a weekend. We spent a week in Portland once when Maria had a conference, stayed at a very nice hotel, pretending to be married, pretending to be rich. And she would tell me secrets, things that Catherine had told her in confidence. Catherine told her once that she had not had a real orgasm in a year, not with me, only fake ones. And Maria told me. We knew it was wrong, that was part of the thrill. Stepping completely outside of regular life, turning the rules on their heads, taking back some part of it for ourselves. Maria would get a boyfriend sometimes and we would stop for a while. We didn't even always stop. Sometimes we kept right on going, right through the boyfriend.

You have no idea the feeling of power that gives you, looking right through the people who think they know you, thinking *I've got a secret.*

Maria was the one who told me Peter had left, left without ever knowing about us. That's what she told me, anyway. That's the trouble with lying: once you start, you don't know where to stop, and she and I had been steeped in lies from the beginning.

I put the food away and carefully wiped the blade of my knife and looked outside again but nothing had changed. The snow fell evenly and without urgency, burying everything beneath it.

I leaned back against the trunk of the largest of the fir trees and closed my eyes. I wondered if I would sleep and, if I did, whether I would wake again. Part of me knew this was foolishness but part of me felt it, the emptiness I fell into, the nothing that was there to receive me. That was the joke: all the rest of it, Maria, Catherine, even Ellie, we had made it all unreal. And this was real, this mountainside, this storm, and it wanted to kill me. This felt ridiculous. That's what I understood, just as I was dropping into sleep: the ridiculous was real, the real ridiculous.

I woke after a while, I didn't know how long. Something had changed, something about the light. The glove had come off my right hand so it lay bare on the ground, but when I awoke it was perfectly warm, which seemed amazing. I looked at my watch and it was five o'clock, much later than I expected it to be. After a minute to clear my head, I stood and looked outside.

There was Idaho, miles below.

The sky was dark and looming low but the land was brilliant white in every direction. Even the gloomy green of the fir trees was covered in white so that it looked like a landscape upside down, with the sky bright below and the earth dark above. I could clearly see the route of the Forest Service trail out. A cold kind of joy welled up in my chest. I was going to live, after all. I remember reading somewhere that simple survival, survival at any cost, was the ethic of the cancer cell. The joy I felt that day was of the same kind: I had beaten the elements. I had won. I had. I. I. I.

I pulled my gaiters on over my boots. It was smart of me to have brought them. My scattered belongings went back in my pack, and I left my resting place behind, feeling a strange nostalgia for that little room of dirt and duff and bark, as if something had happened there.

The day had one last surprise for me: a few steps from my little shelter, no more than ten meters, I came across the un-mistakable paw prints in the snow of a snowshoe hare and her predator, the lynx. In the clean unbroken white of the snow-field, the story was written clearly: the hare's race for cover, the lynx emerging from above and closing the angle, until the two lines of paw prints converged in a bloody patch of snow. A few white scraps of fur were all that was left of the rabbit. A single set of paw prints led away. If I had been awake, if I had been watching through the branches of the fir, I would have seen the animal at long last. I felt a sharp sorrow as a lover would. She had been near me, my prey, my love, and I had missed her by minutes.

I made it back to the truck in an hour, without further in-cident. The truck started fine. It was six-fifteen in the evening. I had three messages on my cell phone.

I shut the truck off again and listened to the stillness all around me. A wind was blowing across the snow, making a big soft sound in the needles of the evergreens. It was half-light, the sky still darker, heavier than the earth. I wanted to stay. It was not too late. I had a change of dry clothes in the back of the truck, a stove, a pair of felt-lined pac boots for standing in the snow. This was where I belonged, out in the wind and the rocks and the trees. Something had happened that day, or almost happened. I wasn't sure what. I was shivering a little, my clothes wet from the walk down through deep snow. I knew the right thing: start the car, drive back down the hill. I wasn't going to get any work done. And I had been lectured about hypothermia enough to respect its ability to kill. A couple of bad decisions, an inch this way or that, and blue-lipped death could be right on you. I had already made my day's worth of bad decisions. I knew what I was supposed to do.

And yet I stayed, as the sky turned black, as the wind slowly filled in the spaces between trees with windblown snow. I waited in the dark and I listened. I knew there would be nothing for me but still I waited and I listened. I heard the wind through the trees. I heard a silence so large that it filled the sky. I heard a branch break under the weight of the new-fallen snow. And once, just after dark—I couldn't be sure—but I thought I heard footsteps.

Burning Bridges, Breaking Glass

R O S S B A C H   S A W   H E R   F I R S T   by accident. He was
not supposed to. But the Healthy Habits meeting was too
much for him that afternoon and so instead he took himself
for a walk up in the canyon behind the Ranch, in the heat of
the day, which the staff advised against. It was more or less a
hundred and the sun beat down through a sky of cloudless flat
blue. At first the desert was barren, stunted with heat; but after a couple of miles in, an hour or so, he started to see things
out of the corner of his eye, little lizards, scattering at his approach, the smell of some herbal plant, even around one corner a tiny green pool of water, crowded with stunted trees that
it took him a moment to recognize as sycamores.

On his way back down in the first cool of the evening, the
shadows lengthening across the flat fragmented rocks, he
missed a turn in the trail somewhere and found himself on

the wrong side of the canyon bottom. It was a steep pitch, a dry cataract, and he didn't much want to bushwhack across it. Neither did he much feel like retracing his steps uphill. He was lost. But there was no need to panic. The canyon could only end up back at the Ranch. It blocked the whole end of the thing, stood solidly between the empty desert and the bright busy suburbs. Rossbach was sure there was a reason for the trail to be on the other side but he felt like he could make it down anyway.

Scratched, stung, sweating, scared, menaced once by a rattlesnake and once by a herd of what seemed to be wild and very stinky miniature pigs, he wandered into the back side of the Ranch forty minutes later. Scared but exhilarated. He had beaten the desert, had forty-five-year-old Rossbach. Fat but undaunted. He was almost sure he had seen a Gila monster.

There he saw her.

She lay prone on a flat padded bench in a small open-air cabana or ramada or whatever they called it here, a round open hut of adobe pillars and tile. Water trickled from a blue tile fountain. The afternoon was still full-on flat heat down in the city but here they felt the first shade of the evening, starting to cool despite the heat radiating off the rocks. The air was a kind of blue.

She was naked from the waist up and presumably from the waist down as well, though she was covered by a towel there. Her face was turned toward him but her eyes were closed—a pretty face, small-featured and pale. Her hair was cut bluntly across the nape of her neck. Blonde, pale, lifeless. A blunt

Mayan-looking attendant was placing smooth black stones at careful intervals along the length of the blonde woman's white spine. The rocks were coming out of a hot bucket, glossy black and wet. Rossbach thought she looked like something to eat, an appetizer. Her decorated body. He stood twenty feet from her naked body and looked at her. He was safe. Nobody would be expecting him here. There were a few kinds of women here at the Ranch and Rossbach wondered what kind she was: a movie star, probably not. Goldie Hawn had been here the week before he came, everybody said so. This girl—this *woman*—looked too young and pretty and sharp to be famous.

Rossbach liked women, liked to type them, to classify and sort according to which kinds he liked and which kinds liked him. Naked was a good start. He liked naked, that's what he would have said, if there had been anyone to listen. In fact he had become cowardly from marriage and from drinking and would only look and talk and tease.

There were a few main kinds of women here: the movie star or ultrarich-type women, who looked fantastic from twenty feet away but catastrophic from up close; the exercise queens, with their faces and asses drawn tight as Christmas bows; the waddling duckling wives and daughters of the Midwestern and suburban well-to-do; and then the few, behind dark glasses, who were here, as Rossbach was, to deal with a little problem. Rossbach tried to construct her body and her face from what he could see through the open portal of the cabana, without much luck. Who are you? he wondered. Naked woman, what could you mean to me?

He had been here for a week and a half, with a week and a half to go.

His last drink—many, many drinks—had been in the Salt Lake airport bar, on the way down.

Just then she opened her eyes and looked directly at him. Rossbach felt a jolt, he had been caught, but it didn't seem to bother her. It was like she didn't see him and after a moment he wondered if she did. The way she lay there languid. None of the black rocks moved, not a sixteenth of an inch. Maybe she wore glasses or contacts and didn't have them. Blind, touching. This was the kind of woman Rossbach liked. The Mayan woman washed her hands and stretched. She was getting ready for something else. After a long moment the blonde woman sighed and closed her eyes again and the Mayan woman touched her gently, softly, on the sides of her neck.

He saw her again the next morning at breakfast. He wondered how many times he had seen her before without noticing. There was nothing wrong with her, she was, in her own way, even beautiful. But she was just another of the doctors' wives, pretty and well educated, moderate in her consumption, sound in body and mind.

He found himself walking behind her on the morning hike. Six in the morning they arose! High into the canyons they climbed! That girl, right behind the leader, Rossbach was almost sure he had seen in a made-for-TV movie, which was strange, as he did not usually watch made-for-TV movies except at three in the morning, and those he did not remember. The blonde girl in front of him was actually prettier in person.

The starlet had the kind of starved, oversized features that the camera loved but this girl, Rossbach thought, would not photograph as well; a fuller face, bigger hips, she'd look chubby on TV. Her nose was a little crooked, too. The kind of thing the rest of them had fixed.

"I'm bored," he said to her when they stopped for their water break.

"Of course you are," she said. She seemed annoyed with him, maybe because he had been looking at her ass. Women knew, and didn't like it. She said, "What were you expecting?"

They were in a little amphitheater of rock, decorated with agave plants and shaded with saguaro cactuses, a sandy oasis. It was still morning, still cool.

"I wasn't expecting much of anything, to tell you the truth," he said.

"And now you've got it," she said, "and now look at you."

"Look at me," he said.

"You can always leave."

"Ah," he said. In fact he could not. The hand of mercy had been extended to him, but he had promised to get himself under control in exchange. Accidents and incidents. He lived in a small town in Montana, a town in which everybody knew everything. He said, "I'm having too much fun to leave."

"I can tell," she said. She grinned and capped her water bottle and turned away to talk with the willowy wife next to her, a sad-faced spaniel blonde, leaving Rossbach with no one. This place was what? A penance, a punishment. He had lost eleven pounds so far, according to the Detecto with the sliding weights in the assessment room. He was clear-eyed and clear-headed and sleeping like a hibernating bear, all except for the dreams, which assaulted him in Technicolor. The night before, he had awakened in the middle of a picnic on the grass with Johnny Cash and Merle Haggard. The future loomed before him in a bright blur.

It's true he had been drinking but not that much. It was just a little slip, an ordinary night that went on longer than he meant it to, a business dinner at the Depot—a question of some mineral rights, a landowner who was trying to buy them back—really just a chance for steaks and red wine, gossip with an old acquaintance from Stanford—then a nightcap in the bar of the Hilton where his friend was staying. It wasn't even that late when he started home, a little past midnight. It had been snowing while they were in the bar, though, snowing secretly. And maybe he did underestimate how slick the streets were, it was almost March, almost spring, he wasn't counting on the way the fresh snow compacted on the frozen street . . . around the corner and just easy as a dream, the Land Cruiser (with its all-wheel-drive and Swedish snow tires) drifting out from under him and around once all the way and then into the Expedition parked on the corner. . . .

Rossbach would do it again anytime if it was legal, that easy glide and total loss of control, the sheer surprise of the thing, and then that *noise*. He loved the sound of breaking glass.

The next thing he knew, Rossbach was in Arizona in front of a half-empty plate, looking across the dining room at the blonde woman and remembering her naked, that line of black stones. . . . The meat was apparently chicken, under a glaze of some sort, garnished with slivers of wild mushroom and bright carrot. They said in Roadmap for Change that the ideal portion of meat was about the size of a deck of cards and ever since he had felt like they were serving him deck after deck, glazed, sauced, sautéed, grilled, pistol-whipped and tied to a chair. . . . A steak, he thought, a porterhouse to fill his plate, and a Napa cabernet, or maybe a Ridge zin.

The blonde woman got up and started across the room and at first it seemed like more than he should believe but no, she was walking straight for him, it was Rossbach she meant to talk to. She leaned down to speak directly and softly in his ear.

"Stop staring at me," she said.

Rossbach felt the blood flush top his face. "I'm sorry," he said, "I . . ."

"Don't worry," she said. "I'll see you after dinner, I'll find you. Just stop looking at me. People will notice."

She stood again and smiled impersonally as if she had just relayed some ordinary piece of information, some fact or appointment. He smiled back, impersonally. The dining room went back to its dim and quiet operations.

Two hours later they sprawled across the single bed, too small for the two of them, in the dim light of her little cell, all rock and bare wood, stripped of ornament, of luxury, even of comfort itself. Rossbach thought that was part of the attraction, one of the things people came here for: to get away from their overfurnished overcomfortable lives. He wondered if it might be possible to get these women to pay to have to dig a ditch or lay track spikes. Rossbach himself had worked one summer on the railroad and still remembered the pink new skin under the blisters. No, he thought. It had to make you slim and it had to make you pretty and it had to give the illusion of suffering without any real suffering.

Karen—her name was Karen—untangled herself from his legs and went across the room in the Arizona moonlight and did something. He couldn't tell what until she came back with a cigarette.

"You really are a beautiful girl," he said.

She shrugged and lit her cig and Rossbach saw something hard in her face in the match light, something bitter.

"Everybody's beautiful here," she said.

"No they aren't."

"Except for the ones who aren't," Karen said. "People like me."

"I just said," he said.

"I heard you," she said. "I mean, there are movie stars here. Models. People who make their living off it, the way they look."

"OK," he said. "For a normal person, you look lovely. Will that do?"

He thought they were just playing a game but then he saw

that she wasn't; she held her palm out toward him to ward him off and took a drag from her cigarette and in the bumblebee light of the coal he saw that she was crying. Rossbach had nothing to say, nothing to bring. He held her naked shoulders to his chest and she let him.

After a moment she blew her nose and said, "It isn't you."

"Well, that's a relief."

She laughed: tight, bitter. She said, "Tell me something."

"OK."

"You do this."

"What?"

"This," she said. She made a gesture: naked, bed, the two of them. He could just make out her body in the dim moonlight but her face was a blur. It wasn't even ten o'clock.

"Not really," he said.

She laughed, again not funny. She asked, "What are you doing here, then?"

"Me? I'm getting my life together, is the story. Getting ready for the next stage. How about you?"

"I'm taking a little break," she said.

He felt an urge to turn away then. He saw her life as she might have seen it herself, small and replaceable. She would have her problems and Rossbach would have to listen to her talk about them: her inability to sleep, her mixed feelings about her husband, even her most closely guarded inner secret, that she was afraid she didn't love her children enough. He didn't know if she had children or not. And really Rossbach had not done this often enough to earn his wings. Still he felt a kind of exhaustion, not looking at her—she was still beautiful in the moonlight—but in the silence between them, the restlessness.

"I came here last winter with my mother-in-law," she said. "You can imagine. She's basically your age but she wants to dress like sisters. Not that your age is bad. I loved it, it was strange how much I loved it. I wasn't expecting anything. Just the weather and the heat and being in my body. You know? I'm not in my body, not so much, I'm all in my head. And then I got home and it was a problem, you know? It was kind of a problem, how much I liked this place. I felt like the end of summer vacation. Suddenly I'm back in Kettering, Ohio. I'm talking too much, aren't I?"

"You're all right."

"It's what I do, I just talk and talk until I get a thing figured out. And right now I just feel really strange, you know? It's not your fault. I think you're a beautiful man, I do. I just feel really strange, like I'm not even myself. I feel like a stranger in my own skin."

"I can go, if you want me to."

"Maybe you should," she said. She untangled herself, rose and walked to the open window, stubbed her cigarette out in an open soda can. She had the premium room, the one that looked out over the open desert, away from the city, away from the rest of the Ranch. Elf owls, rattlesnakes, coyotes watched her nakedness, along with Rossbach.

"I'm not a hundred percent," she said. "I don't want to hurt your feelings."

"You're not going to hurt my feelings," he said; though she

already had, some insubstantial little disappointment. Some part of him had wanted to sleep with another body next to his, her small, neat body. Some part of him had expected this.

They met the next night after dinner, too, and went back to her little cell for an hour.

Rossbach felt something strange happening within himself, some new thing trying to come out. His *qi*, is what they called it. His *qi* was all fucked up, according to Hope, the Chinese-medicine-and-Alexander-technique teacher. He was blocked in every vein and artery. The acupressure and massage were starting to loosen things up, she said, and maybe Rossbach was starting to believe in this. Certainly when he made love with Karen he felt limber and energized, maybe from all the fresh air and exercise and not drinking but maybe his *qi* was starting to come around as well. Really he didn't know what it was. Rossbach had assumed, when he came to the Ranch, that he would take his punishment and behave well, lie low until the whole thing blew over and then go back to being himself. Rossbach liked himself, the prow of his belly, the forward push of his mustache. He liked to drink and he thought he was good at it, it brought out the laughter in him, which was sometimes hard to find otherwise. Rossbach had never seriously considered a life in which he did not drink.

These last few days, though—two weeks into the cure, and Karen ever always at the edge of his sight—he felt that there might be some other life, some other possibility. Lying naked on the mat while some burly girl worked over his shoulders and then his central back and his spine. He felt things

releasing, poisons leaving his body. He didn't miss the hang-
overs much, nor the boozy bullshitty conversation. Something
was happening in his body, some force or energy, maybe the
Chinese were right. He felt it when he was with her, a force
or energy that originated at a spot halfway between his navel
and his dick, a place a couple of inches deep inside the skin of
his belly. He felt alive and energized as a man who woke up to
find that his house was on fire.

That third night, she said to him, "That first time I was
here with my mother-in-law, I was so jealous. Everybody cou-
pling up and heading off into the bushes. In the end it was me
and her and about seven old ladies playing canasta."

"No one has ever played canasta here."

"How do you know?"

"No one has ever been old here, either. At least not from
ten feet away."

"You know everything, don't you?"

"Maybe."

She slapped him across the cheek, playfully it seemed, but
harder than she needed to. Maybe harder than she meant to.
It hurt.

"I was trying to tell you something," she said. "Pushy guys,
pushy pushy guys. What is it with me and pushy guys?"

He slapped her on her bare bottom, hard enough to sting
a little.

"What was that?" she said.

"Revenge," said Rossbach. "I'm big on revenge."

"You'll block yourself all up again," she said. "Hope was

just telling me all about it. Anger just bottles everything up, gets it stuck in the wrong places. You'll get your *qi* all blocked up in your head and then you'll get cancer. Do you believe any of this shit?"

"I don't have to," Rossbach said. "I just do it and it makes me feel better."

"Ah," she said, "the body knows."

The next night, Saturday night, was Karen's last at the Ranch. The next day she would be back in Kettering, Ohio. They snuck out of the Ranch—it was simple as calling a cab, nobody was keeping track—and went to the Hacienda del Sol, the House of the Sun, where they sat in a white adobe dining room beneath red velvet curtains and portraits of Mexican imperial dignitaries. Home and not-home, Rossbach thought. After long consideration he ordered the cowboy T-bone and a bottle of Duckhorn Rector Creek cabernet.

"Give me a minute," Karen said to the waiter. He went to fetch the wine and she continued to peer at the menu through her stylish, small black glasses. She was, he thought, a fundamentally serious person. In the candlelight she looked much younger, a little unsure, a little out of place. Without looking up from the menu she said, "A place like this, I feel sometimes like it's just all butter, like no matter what I order it's just going to be a stick of butter on my plate."

"That's kind of the point."

"Sometimes it sounds better than other times. I've been liking myself here."

The waiter came back with bottle and towel, went through the ritual of defoiling and decorking and the holy sip. Karen watched him as he raised the glass to his lips. He could smell the alcohol in it, like aftershave. It had been a couple of weeks. The wine itself was inky and tannic, too closed, but it would open up.

"Fine," said Rossbach, and the waiter poured for both of them, and Karen ordered the swordfish Veracruzana. It felt odd to be amid such luxury. Karen looked at home here—her husband was an eye-nose-throat doc, they had spent their time in white-tablecloth places—and at the same time strange. He was used to seeing her against the backdrop of tan rock, the sound of dripping water. He was used to seeing her naked.

"You look good in clothes," he said.

"Ha!" she said. "Thank you. I guess."

"I don't want you to leave," he said.

But it sounded so much like the thing he ought to say, the line from the script, that they both were embarrassed. They folded their napkins into their laps. They looked around at the other diners, the little courtyard that the dining room wrapped around with its gravel walkways and dry fountain.

"You don't like the wine," she said.

"It needs to open up a little," he said. "It needs to breathe."

She sipped at her glass and made a face. It was leathery, closed, tannic, harsh.

"You don't like it," Rossbach said. "We can get you a white, next time he comes by."

"I'm all right with water, for now," she said.

They were strange to each other, people who didn't belong together here. It was the room or the food or the wine. She was just going to go home and so was Rossbach, though not for a week or so. It was strange to be so much in his element and yet so out of place. Rossbach belonged here, he knew it. He just didn't feel it at this moment.

"Oh, Christ, Bill," Karen said.

"What?"

"There's no place in this whole round world for us, is there?"

Rossbach didn't have an answer. It was strange, he knew himself to be older, more experienced in the world if not exactly wiser—you couldn't call Rossbach wise, not with a straight face—and he should have been able to teach her, to tell her. But he couldn't find anything in himself that felt right; fell back upon the smartass. He said, "We could be back at the Ranch eating carrot sticks."

"That's not what I meant."

"Hitting that last Where's the Joy? session."

"Don't be a bastard."

"I'm not trying to be."

She brightened, suddenly, the mood passing. "You don't strike me as the kind of man who needs to try," she said. "It seems like bastardy might come naturally to you."

"Bastardy," he said. "Nice word."

"I was an English major," she said.

"Still," he said. Rossbach tried the wine again: still tight, some unpleasant combination of leather and ink. There was bread, and real butter. Conversation sparkled all around them while they sat sipping their water. He said, "You should come to Montana sometime. Come in the summer, it's really pretty there in the summer."

"That would be awesome," she said. "I could meet your wife."

"I was just making conversation."

"I know," she said. "Just trying to get along."

"Are you in a bad mood?"

"I don't know what I am. Restless, I guess. I'm going to be in Ohio tomorrow. Have you ever been in Ohio in March?"

"It can't be worse than Montana."

"Oh, yes it can."

"All the dog turds, all winter long they've been lying in the snow," he said. "They all defrost at once in everybody's yard. Plus everybody's crazy crazy crazy from being inside all winter."

"Lucky us," she said. But Rossbach couldn't tell how she meant it.

Just then the waiter came and both of them started to laugh. The cowboy steak looked like a whale flipper or a dismembered arm, flopping over the sides of the wide oval platter, and the Veracruzana would easily feed a family of four. A secondary waiter came up bearing a secondary platter of fixings for Rossbach, his horseradish and fried potatoes on a separate plate. It was like a dream of food, a concert where you didn't have any clothes onstage and didn't know the music anyway. Rossbach couldn't begin to imagine what to do.

He took a bite and it was fatty and charred and smoky, vile in its excess.

Lovely Karen laughed at him and she was right, she was right to laugh.

"What do you want to do?" she said.

"We should go," he said. "Do you want to? I feel like we should go."

"All right," she said. "No, perfect."

Forty minutes later they were in the canyon behind the Ranch, walking out into the open desert by moonlight. It was so clear here! The moonlight cast hard shadows on the rock walls of the canyon, the spiky century plants and the tall manlike saguaros. It reminded Rossbach of the day-for-night of the cowboy movies of his youth, Roy and Dale sneaking through some cactus-strewn pass to head off the rustlers. Rossbach had traded his going-out-to-dinner clothes for rugged sneakers and shorts but Karen was still in her little dress and Keds. He let her walk ahead, so that he could catch her when she slipped, every few minutes. The cool wind was blowing down the canyon, out of the forests higher up, the mountains that rose all the way to running water and pine trees.

They came to a rock the size of a car, or even a little bigger, a round, smooth dome that projected from a little rise. The front was smooth, impregnable, but a scatter of loose rock had fallen against the back side and they were able to climb up there. It was remarkable how smooth the rock was on top, water-worn for years, for centuries. How long had this rock been there waiting for them? The stars wheeled above them like performing bees. The chandelier city spread out, miles below them, like the devil's bargain that it was. Rossbach laughed again at the thought of all that beautiful food and Karen laughed with him, knowing. The other thing that was remarkable about that rock was how much of the day's heat it still held, warm to the touch. Warm and smooth. There was no one here to see—they would have heard them—and nowhere to go from here but back to the Ranch, to town, to the airport, to their separate lives. . . .

Karen was on top of him and he meant to spare her but the clothes he had laid down slipped out to the side in the moment and she skinned her knee on the rock. She sat cross-legged and naked and tried to look at it in the moonlight. But all either of them could see was a trickle of black blood running down.

"That's going to be hard to explain," she said, touching herself gingerly.

"You tripped when you were on a hike," he said. "You fell down on a rock."

"That's right," she said. "I forgot. You just lie, is all."

"Sorry," he said.

"No, I just . . ."

She waved the conversation away with her hand, fumbled

in her clothes and found her cigarettes and her little Bic lighter. Her face was all in tatters when she lit up, eggs and oysters. A thing his grandmother used to say.

"It's nothing wrong with you," she said. "I'm not complaining. It's just, I don't know, a failure is all. I'm not supposed to want this."

"But you do."

"Do I?"

"Why are you angry with me?"

"I'm not angry. I can be angry without being angry at you."

She puffed furiously at her cigarette, lighting the space between them with the orange glow of the coal, the moonlit luxury of her skin. Rossbach himself felt solid and slim after two weeks here, tight and easy. Bodies and bodies. She came expecting to do exactly this, a little adventure, a week away and a body not her husband's. She had practically said so. Now she seemed upset with him. This was not fair, it was not just, but Rossbach did not expect fairness from her. He had come to accept this sense of injustice as the price he had to pay for the company of women. They were not reasonable creatures but lovely.

"You can't help it," he said. "You want what you want. It's not complicated."

"Until it is," she said.

"That's right."

The next morning she was gone. The airport van left at quarter after five; Rossbach was still awake, he heard the tires on the gravel as she left. Karen hadn't slept either. He felt like an alias of himself. Not just tired, although he was tired as he had ever been. But to be here without her and all these zombies in their leotards. He fought a sense of unreality all through the day, unreal the tiny, carefully crafted meals, unreal the group session, the hike where the two of them had been naked not twelve hours before and the pretty, surgically altered brunette from La Jolla who wanted to talk to him. It was a world haunted by plastic flesh-colored robots.

On Sunday evenings from five till eight they gave the continuing guests their cell phones back while the newcomers were getting settled. Rossbach checked his list of missed calls and his messages and his e-mail but there was nothing from Karen.

She would have been home for hours.

Maybe the flight was delayed.

Something strange came out of Rossbach that week, a side of himself that he had not known was there. He couldn't stand to be among the others, the polite and self-absorbed, the preening narcissists and hopeless heavies, all that good hair and well-tended teeth and workout clothes in colors like leather and sphagnum and autumn oak. . . . He went feral, did Rossbach. He stayed to himself up in the canyons, learned to stay still long enough to see the rattlesnakes, which were coiled on every ledge, sleeping in every shadow. Twice he saw a Gila monster, though he never saw either one move, and they were close enough to the same spot—Rossbach was mildly lost almost all the time—that they might have been the same one, and it might have been dead. He saw javelinas and bats and once at sunset an elf owl perched in the high top of a tall saguaro. And always the city down below, mindlessly endlessly busy. And always the Ranch at the end of the canyon, serene, expensive.

Still he did not drink.

One night at dinner he overheard a television producer refer to his sobriety as if it were another person standing in the room. He said, "I really felt that she was endangering my *sobriety*," and after that it was like there were three of them in the room all the time, Rossbach drunk and Rossbach dry and then Rossbach's sobriety. He took his sobriety with him everywhere, unwillingly, like a country cousin, or the child of your parents' friends, in town for a week and dumped on you to entertain.... The week alone went on and on. On Wednesday he took a cab to a huge, fantastic mall with Rolls-Royces and Ferraris in the parking lot and went directly to the Verizon kiosk and checked his e-mail and his messages but there was nothing from her.

Karen was gone, just gone. He went into Williams-Sonoma and bought his wife a French enamel stove. The stove itself was $8300 and delivery was going to be another $1300. He put it on his credit card. A little surprise. It was called the La Cornue and Rossbach wondered if that had anything to do with a unicorn.

The minutes crawled by like wounded ants. The hours, the days.

Sunday came at last and Rossbach and his sobriety flew to Montana. Past the airport bars he walked, resolute. But circling over Helena he saw the gray hills, the scraps of snow and dirt, a mountain spring of cold and mud and gray skies and he knew that temporary spring, the one he had visited so far south, was over. Summer was still two months away and winter long gone and this nothing in between. There was no message from Karen. He slept with his wife. It didn't seem like there was anything to wait for.

They lived a little ways outside of town, in a canyon on a creek, back up in the trees. In the night, when he couldn't sleep, Rossbach would watch the deer come down out of the hills to drink from the creek. The snow was off the grass, down in the bottoms anyway, and the deer could graze again. But the grass was brown and winter-killed and it seemed like the deer were just holding on, sketchy and skeletal. They looked like shadows in the moonlight, gray on black. Still he did not drink.

He knew where she lived, which clubs she belonged to, her time in the Fourth of July Fun Run 5K. Twenty-four minutes: fast. She had been honored by the March of Dimes. He saw what he believed to be the roof of her house, as seen from space. She did not call or send a message. Nor did Rossbach to her.

A Saturday night in May, a night of oceanic rain and cloud and wind, a low-pressure front blowing in from the Pacific, Rossbach sat in the dark in the bay windows at the back of the house, waiting to see if the deer would come that night and listening to the flap of plastic sheeting in the breeze—they had to blast through part of the kitchen wall to fit the fucking unicorn in, the worst idea he had in years. The hole was patched with lath and plastic, waiting for carpenters who wouldn't come. She was on Eastern time, three-thirty in the morning. She would have come home from a party a little drunk. She would have taken her earrings off. He could feel her, out there in the dark.

Rossbach got up to fix himself a little drink.

Every kind of liquor in the cabinet, why throw it away? They could serve it at their parties and besides, his wife liked a little drink once in a while, usually a glass of white wine but sometimes gin. She wasn't the one with the problem. Rossbach understood, looking into the liquor cabinet, that this had been a mistake. But it was too late to stop now. He thought, Come to Papa.

In the end he settled on a scotch on the rocks. A drink of elegance and sophistication. The very thing he had been missing.

He sat in the bay window for a few minutes with the ice melting in his glass.

In the end he threw it in the sink. A week later he was flying into Dayton. It was June in Ohio, full glorious spring with flowers bursting out of the driveway beds and bees everywhere. Rossbach had forgotten. He had grown up in Michigan himself and all he remembered was the flat, tobacco-colored sunlight and the color of that yellow brick you saw everywhere. That and fireflies was summer. That and dirty snow. But this fullness, this bee-loud-buzzing, pink-and-purple spring he had forgotten.

He drove his rented Camry through his childhood. It was

a warm Saturday and children were riding skateboards and playing basketball. The curbs and gutters were the same dirty tan as Michigan. Men were drinking beer as they washed their American cars. His heart was crying *mistake, mistake* but again it was too late to stop.

Karen lived in an older part of town, a street of tall ugly houses set back in trees, surrounded by broad lawns and deep shady porches. Minivans and John Kerry bumper stickers, once in a while the old showplace with a Cadillac parked out front but Hondas and Toyotas for the most part, children's toys in the yards, recycling bins. The young and the affluent lived here. It was strange to think that they had problems here, that Rossbach himself was somebody's problem. It was very strange to see that this whole imaginary life of Karen-without-him was in fact real and that he in fact should just drive his ass back to the airport and abandon this folly while stone was left upon stone. He understood that he himself represented an outbreak of the unreal, the chaotic, the dream life intruding upon the daylit one.

He parked and waited for her to come out. A crew of Mexican or Central American men in straw hats drove up in a van, towing a trailer of mowers and machinery, and cut and trimmed the lawn in minutes. It was startling how quickly they worked. The husband paid them through the door but Rossbach could not see his face.

She came out looking American and clean in pastel shorts and pink T-shirt. He felt pity for her. She had frosted her hair with platinum since Arizona. He knew he should just go, he should leave her alone. Rossbach was chaos itself. He was violence upon her.

He followed her to the parking lot of the Fresh Fields and then he did not have the nerve to approach her and then he followed her inside. After the bright afternoon, it was dim and damp inside, smelled of vegetables and dirt. She came around the end cap of the produce section and he was standing there with his hands at his sides.

"Oh, fuck," she said, scared.

"I'm sorry," he said.

"No," she said, and then she was embracing him and on him and immediately weeping, he could feel the tears through the fabric of his shirt. "I didn't expect you," she said.

"Do you want me to go?" he said. "I can go if you want."

"You'd better," she said.

She pulled away from him and then they were just two strangers facing each other in the produce section. Her face was a mess. Eggs and oysters, Rossbach thought.

"You came all this way," she said. "Just for this."

Suddenly he was the one who felt empty-handed, embarrassed. It was, he thought, unkind of her to ask when she already must know the answer.

"I did," he said.

"I can't give up my life for you," she said. "I'm sorry."

Still she didn't turn away. She stood at arm's length regarding him, his face, his body, trim and useless. All those hours in the gym, all that good sense and moderation, all for nothing, he thought. All for *you.*

"OK," she said. "I have to go."

Rossbach was a *fool.* He understood this sharply, all at once. A fool's errand. He thought he understood but he didn't, not at all. At least he was a long way from home, in a place where nobody knew him.

"All right, then," he said. But he couldn't bring himself to leave.

She wouldn't leave either. She was waiting for him. A Mexican standoff, Rossbach thought. Just go.

"Karen?" It was a long, tall girl, a runner from the looks of her, a friend of Karen's. Probably another doctor's wife. "Karen, are you all right?"

And this, this last: a long look, a helplessness, a door closing. He was not wrong. There was nothing to hope for but he had not been wrong about her.

"I'm fine," she said to her friend, and turned away, walked away with her cart in front of her and her friend beside her.

He went the short way out the front door so she wouldn't have to look at him again, out of the restrained light and into the bright bee-loud afternoon of full spring. Cherry trees in the parking lot blossomed in pink, snowing pink and white petals onto the cars parked beneath them. Rossbach sweated in his long pants and presentable shirt. Children kissed in the park, drinking cool wine from the bottle. Ohio men gassed their cars, racing down the boulevards in the roar of oil and speed and tire smoke. Everyone in the whole round world was kissing and fucking, everyone but him.

Rossbach bought a fifth of Bombay gin, a quart of tonic water and three limes at the liquor store on the strip by his hotel. Rossbach was a man who liked his limes. It was a Saturday and the hallways of the Red Lion were strolled by wet children in bathing suits who left their footprints behind them in the carpet. His room smelled of freeway and chlorine. The interstate whizzed by a hundred yards outside his window: Cincinnati, Indianapolis, Columbus, Chicago. That same tan or yellow brick of his childhood, everywhere outside his window.

Four o'clock.

By six o'clock he had still not made up his mind. The fifth sat unopened atop the television set, which was playing baseball with the sound off, Reds and Mets. His sobriety. Rossbach decided to take his sobriety out for a walk but when he got downstairs he found it oppressively hot, even in shorts, and there was nothing to walk to, and the smell of car exhaust and oil smoke filled the air. Poor people lived here and drove their cars with worn-out leaking rings and bad mufflers. The Red Lion sat in a triangle of concrete, surrounded by the freeway, by a major mall on the second side and an Office Depot and ten-plex theater on the third. In between was no-man's-land, trash and asphalt.

Inside was cleaner and quieter but no better.

He had a flight out at noon the next day, which meant—he sat on the edge of the bed, trying to make sense of himself— that he *knew* he would fail at this, would make a fool of himself. Then why? The full hot knowledge of spring came in the window with the evening sunlight, the scent of flowers and tar, green grass and french-fry grease. He lay back on the bed, atop the slick polyester satin of the bedspread, and he felt himself in his body. He felt younger now than when he had been drinking, slimmer and stronger. He remembered days at seventeen of just feeling himself in his body, the spring of it, the miracle. Somewhere inside Rossbach was still seventeen, worn and frayed but the green fuse still lit in him, the spark. Confused as a dog with two dicks. Lost in Ohio.

She came at nine-thirty.

He knew all along she would. He was certain of her. Except that he did find himself in tears as he held her, and Rossbach never cried. Just a little. A leak.

She held him at arm's length and looked at him and he at her: pretty, worn, older than he remembered her. Her eyes looked tired. Over her shoulder, himself in the mirror—elephant-eyed, the eyes of old Rembrandt, tired but *clear*—and the two of them together. The great canoe paddle of his hand. What did she see in him?

Something.

She looked from his face to the bottle, unopened on the desk. She said, "You didn't."

"I didn't."

"Why not?" she asked. "You had every excuse."

"I didn't feel like it."

"You knew I was coming."

"Maybe," he said. Then cut the light and the TV set, peeled

back the cool sheets on the bed—the air still bearing exhaust and roses through the open window—took off her blouse and shorts, her socks and underwear, laid her down in the open bed and took his own clothes off and lay down beside her and it was more than he could contain, he felt it spilling out of him again, his *qi*, whatever, naked, connected.

Afterward they lay naked and Rossbach could feel the earth turning under them, the naked rock. He said, "I'm not suited to this. Not at all. I'm not an adventurous person at heart."

"Look at me," she said. "A doctor's wife. All the safe choices."

"Where are you right now?"

"I'm nowhere."

"You just left?"

"I couldn't think of anything," she said. "I was afraid you might leave. I didn't even know where you were! I've been sitting in my car with the cell phone and my phone book, I've been calling every hotel and motel in town. It's a good thing I'm a snoop."

"What?"

"I got your last name from the office," she said. "Before I left the Ranch."

"I told you my name."

"You never did. I had to sneak it for myself."

"I'm sorry," he said.

"It's all right."

"No, I'm sorry," he said. He was again embarrassed. He

said, "I'm such a clumsy person. I hurt people when I don't mean to."

"And sometimes when you do."

"And sometimes when I do," he said. "I'm not a perfect person, not at all. You didn't really think I'd leave, did you?"

"I didn't think you'd come in the first place."

"You didn't?"

"I didn't *know.*"

"Well," he said. "Now you know."

"I can't leave my children," she said.

"We'll figure something out," he said. And though she didn't believe him, she curled against him, kissed his shoulder, pretended to rest in the gathering dark, the soft flesh shadows. Rest, he thought, and she closed her eyes. He thought of gray ghostly deer coming down to the creek to drink, grazing on the dead brown grass. He thought of the hole in the side of his house, patched and ragged. This was not that. He kissed her little breasts. Through the open window came the perfume of a Midwestern spring, gasoline and roses and tar, the sounds of people gunning it in the distance, the constant hiss of the interstate, the sounds of breaking glass and laughter, the sound of life itself.

Acknowledgments

I'd like to thank the MacDowell Colony for their kind and vital support.

A Note About the Author

KEVIN CANTY is the award-winning author of the novels *Into the Great Wide Open*, *Nine Below Zero*, and *Winslow in Love*, as well as the short-story collections *Honeymoon and Other Stories* and *A Stranger in This World*. His work has been published in *The New Yorker, Esquire, GQ, Details, The New York Times Magazine, Tin House* and *Glimmer Train*. He lives and writes in Missoula, Montana.

A NOTE ABOUT THE TYPE

Where the Money Went is set in Epic, a contemporary font designed by Neil Summerour of TypeTrust, a type foundry dedicated to maintaining the value and humanity of typographic practice.

Two years went into the making of Epic, a serif with subtle letterform construction based on sixteenth- and seventeenth-century French and Venetian garaldes.